THE GUNS OF HIGH MEADOW

The fugitive had planned so carefully that, until he had covered almost three states, the people who wanted him back in Montana had no idea which direction he'd taken.

Then he rode into Mandan, Colorado, to have a stolen horse shod, he was apprehended for horsestealing, a blizzard nearly buried the town cutting it off from the rest of the world, and a hate-filled stage company manager who wanted only dead outlaws in his town, schemed to have the fugitive lynched.

Ed Teel, town marshal of Mandan, took the fugitive with him to save a lost and injured traveller. The very next day all hell broke loose, Ed was branded an outlaw, along with the fugitive, as was the man they had rescued, and only desperation and fast guns kept him alive until it was possible to set things to rights again.

THE GUNS OF HIGH MEADOW

THE GUNS OF HIGH MEADOW

by
Buck Standish

MAGNA PRINT BOOKS
Long Preston, North Yorkshire,
England.

British Library Cataloguing in Publication Data.

Standish, Buck, *1916—*
   The guns of High Meadow.
   Rn: Lauran Paine

   ISBN 1-85057-903-2

First Published in Great Britain by Robert Hale Ltd., 1973

Copyright © 1973 and 1982 by Robert Hale Ltd.

Published in Large Print 1990 by arrangement with Robert Hale
Ltd., London.

Printed and bound in Great Britain by
Redwood Burn Limited, Trowbridge, Wiltshire.

CONTENTS

CONTENTS

CHAPTER 1

A Lay of Land

It was an old night, the moon was full which meant the month was nearly finished. The last few mornings, there had been a skiff of frost on the grass and sedge, with a rind of ice wherever he encountered water. It was coldest before dawn and the great rusty moon crossed heaven on a line between two mountain peaks.

Lately, too, there was a ghostly low fog, transparent and cloying, in the marshy places. Summer was gone and autumn would not linger long. It never did, in the highlands, because deep winter was impatient. The Indians called this the Time Of Turning Leaves. Later, it would be the Time Of Long Sleep, but by then he intended to be far southward because a solitary mounted man could not survive a highland winter unless he had a cabin, cords of firewood and a store of food, things he did not have and could not get.

Montana was a bitterly cold place in winter, nor was it much better in autumn, but he was almost to the Wyoming line, which was encouraging, except that the season was also advancing southward; they were travelling about neck-and-neck. Any day now the first blizzard could arrive. That would finish him. He knew it, and drove himself harder than he drove his horse, worrying about it.

Instinct told him to stay to the lowest elevations, which he did when he could, but once a man left Montana's grasslands there were tiers upon tiers of mountains. If he got caught in that kind of a maze when the blizzard struck, folks might not even find his bones for years to come.

That thought rode his spirit hard each time he felt the keening wind rising at his back, out of the north, as he rode from a stony parapet towards the lower country on southward, and when he was at last clear of the mountains, each time he gave silent thanks, then felt troubled that the next mountain-bulwark would be his final place.

Hunting was poor this late in the season. Nor dared he try for meat close to the stacks of hay or buildings he passed wraithlike in the clear, cold nights; one gunshot and more men would be after him.

The last horse he had stolen had, upon dawn-light inspection, turned out to be sturdy, but old. Someone's retired cowhorse, probably.

Every freezing morning when he saddled up and rode along, it took the honest old horse an hour to warm out of his stiffness. He was willing, but he had served his time and now he tired easily.

Over the line in Wyoming, the horse slowed because it had to, which meant its rider might be losing in his race with winter, so he deviated from the arrow-straight southerly course in the Yellowstone vicinity, scouted for a ranch, and when he found one he spent a whole day lying in timber like an Indian, watching the buildings, the corrals and barns, and the habit of the people down there as they came and went. Harvest time of year folks pulled the shoes off their horses before turning them out. They filled root-cellars with potatoes and pumpkins and tinned food in ranks upon rough plank shelves. They sanded the runners on sleighs and made firewood by the cord. They worked like squirrels, but mostly they stayed close to their towns and ranches. Riders no longer worked the ranges; mostly, the hired hands had been paid off and by now were southward where real winter could not reach.

He was sorry for the old horse, so he took him down to a haystack, pulled aside the logs so the horse could stand in close and be protected from the knifing north wind while he ate his fill.

Then he went back to the tree where he had the new horse snubbed with a lariat and put on the frayed blanket, the weighty saddle, and the little, stiff grazing bit.

It was always with a sense of adventure that he mounted fresh animals. A man could hardly ask an owner the disposition of the horse he was stealing. With old horses there was never much doubt, but younger animals were like people; it took a lot of close association to really know them.

This time, the horse did not offer to pitch or run or bite, but it walked a mile with a hump in its back from the icy saddleblanket, acting like it would fire with its new rider. Then it settled down and turned out to be one of those rare horses that could walk a hole in the daylight. It was solid bay with a skimpy mane and tail and the barrel and lengthy legs of a thoroughbred, at least of a thoroughbred-cross. And it also turned out to like company. For two days it would not let the man out of its sight, and even afterwards, when it was in new country with other things to interest it, the horse would not stray from the man's meagre camp.

The only thing it refused to do was carry bloody meat. When the fugitive shot a young she-goat on a mountainside, carved out the saddle and hams and wanted to then get away from that place as soon as possible because someone might have heard the gunshot and ride over out of curiosity, the bay horse shied and reared and snorted and rolled his eyes. That smell of blood was terrifying to him even though he trusted the man who was trying to tie meat to the saddle.

In the end, the man could take only a small part of his kill, and had to be satisfied with that as he loped on southward.

What had been a time of no-moon after crossing into Wyoming, became a time of some-moon, then quarter-moon and half-moon. The bay horse was a fleeing man's succour, his answer to a prayer, if he'd ever prayed. It kept its round rump to the oncoming face of winter as though it knew, too, what kind of a long chance it was taking each time it topped out over a windswept stony rim, and headed straight down through the twisted, gravelly canyons always southward. The man came to respect the horse, then to like it, and finally to joke with it and confide in it, and treat it as a lot more than a horse.

But the best horses go tender, especially after crossing nearly the full flinty distance of Wyoming, after climbing goat trails over slickrock, and ploughing through the grit and abrasive shale of miles-long canyons.

Ordinarily, the man would have done as he'd done so often before; find a place where there were other horses, stalk one, leave his tender-footed bay and keep right on going with a new animal under the frayed blanket and scarred saddle.

When the horse went willingly, but took crimped steps on his bruised feet and flinched from every sharp stone, the man knew better than to listen when the thought arrived; knew better because his entire strategy thus far had been to avoid people and ranches, and of course towns. But the horse had to be shod or abandoned. So far, this was the best animal he'd had under him. That was not the whole reason for the man's argument with himself. The world was full of good, sound horses, but the man was a loner, a quiet individual who had always stayed apart and now had more reason than ever to remain that way.

The horse had come to fill a void in the man. It was as though they were conspirators together, friends and even more than just friends.

Another argument favouring the horse was that this far southward one solitary stranger travelling through some town needing shoes for his horse, shouldn't raise a ripple. At least the man told himself this even when his fixed ideas militated against going anywhere near a village or a ranch, because no matter how far or long a man travelled, if there was sufficient reason for other men to do it, they would be doggedly coming down his backtrail.

In the end, the man decided in favour of the bay horse. He knew better even when he did it; knew perfectly well he was yielding to the weakness that lived in every fugitive.

His careful plan had been to do exactly as he had done; move ahead of winter but just far enough ahead so that those who might be following, would get cold and held back when the snows fell. He had ridden himself down, had not been really warm nor comfortable since the last time he'd been inside a warm building up in Montana, but the cold, the haste, the sleeplessness and even the occasional hunger, had been deliberate. And so far they had been in the man's favour. Had been his price to pay.

It was, he told the horse, an outside risk, and if it did not pan out, then everything the man had gone through before would have been for nothing, which would be one hell of a disaster after all the planning and discomfort and wearing-down he had gone through. On the other hand, the outside risk was not actually very great, not so far southward, and anyway he was tired of stealing horses that, until now, had never been up to his demands on them. He was better-mounted than he had ever been before, and that counted for something.

He began angling eastward across foothills and valleys in search of a road that would lead to a town. It was easier for the horse when they reached a high meadow where the grass lay curled and matted and brown from killing frosts. It was like walking across a carpet. The horse stepped out in his customary mile-eating walk again, and the man smiled, unwilling to heed the warning in the back of his mind.

When they found a road, though, the man turned wolflike with wariness. He had been allying himself with trees since childhood, and on this southward run he had kept to that alliance, lying still and patient like an Indian watching with a hard, quick interest everything he saw, but mostly people and their settlements.

The road he found ran through an aspen stand, past a great, grey pillar-rock, then down towards a clump of winter-cowed buildings that let it part them until it went due southward out beyond, and down towards a dawn-misted distant lift of upland mountains forming the southernmost bulwark of the plateaux. It was an old road and so was that clutch of weathered buildings it bisected. They looked squatty and ugly in the icy dawn, without any daylight to brighten or soften their functional uniformity.

As the man lay in stiff discomfort among the white-barked aspens, and as he saw the brittle pre-dawn pale out towards sunrise, little smoke-streamers rose here and there from chimneys and kitchen stovepipes. The women-folk in their warm and spicy-scented kitchens would be brewing coffee, carving off breakfast meat, maybe even fluffing up a batter of biscuits.

Sometimes a man paid a God-awful price for the things he deliberately did.

When the sun came without heat but with dazzling brilliance, the fugitive studied the land roundabout, which was empty even of cattle. He also saw, and studied a long while, a heavy grey cloud-wall that lay partially hidden like a smokebank during a forest fire, just beyond the farthest northward rims. He had got out of Montana, had crossed Wyoming, was balanced on the line between Wyoming and Colorado, and back there was the first storm of winter. It did not seem to be moving but the man knew how deceptive nature was.

He got to his feet and went back through the trees to the bay horse. He might lose his race after all, but one thing he knew for a fact, unless he got shoes on the horse he could not possibly even come close to winning it.

He mounted and rode out of the aspens to the stage-road, then southward at a walk towards the stirring town, the first one he had visited in a long while, and with any kind of good fortune, the last one he would have to visit again for an even longer while.

CHAPTER 2

One Flaw

Hanging high in an aspen tree completely obscured from the ground, the fugitive had left his saddlebags with the intention of coming back for them. It had been a reasonable precaution, but as he rode towards the road, then down it, he felt as though he had abandoned a friend, had ridden away from the key to all that was good and pleasing in life. It made him more inward than ever, to do that, but he clove to his logic and did not even glance back until he was nearing the upper end of the town, where a rotting sign said, 'Mandan—Population Three Hundred.' Below that glowing statistic some cowboy had written, 'including prairie dogs'. The man smiled, looked back towards the aspens, then squared up and entered town with a little, low-flowing cold wind at his back.

Mandan was one of those back-country villages where the law also operated a liverybarn and where the proprietor of the general store was the postmaster, and, in Mandan, the

19

undertaker. It had a schoolhouse out back of town to the west. It had a saloon, a stage office, and between the general mercantile establishment and the gunsmith's shop, was a cubbyhole telegraph office. There was a forge, which was where the stranger drew rein and dismounted as a thick man with a russet beard cursed at a sticking door, badly battered and sagging, that grudgingly opened to reveal the inside of his sooty blacksmith's shop.

As though the stranger were an acquaintance the blacksmith finished with the door and turned to say, 'Someday I'm going to knock that damned thing loose and build me a new one.' He studied the bay horse's feet with merry blue eyes, then looked upwards at the stranger. 'I been saying that for eight years. Well sir, what can I do for you? A new set all around?'

The stranger nodded and turned to remove the saddle. 'Looks like winter over yonder, to the north-east,' he said, lifting the saddle and upending it in the dust out front.

The smith was tying his muleskin apron into place. 'Soon now,' he concurred. 'You headin' south? If a feller can get off the highlands and down into New Mexico in time, he won't suffer much, but once the blizzards hit them mountains between here and there, it's damned miserable travelling. Well, lead him inside and we'll nail 'em on.'

The smith had to stir fresh life into his forge and tramp the treadle to get the draught set, but because he never let the coals die this only took a few minutes. Then he picked up a front foot of the bay horse and worked with rasp and knife. 'Tender,' he said, bending over the hoof. 'Not much trimming to do on this one.' As the smith straightened up to go across towards the wall where rows of cold shoes hung on pegs according to size, he said, 'Calks or plates, mister?'

Plates would be satisfactory. If a man had to run a horse hard calked shoes could be an impediment. The stranger said, 'Plates'll be fine,' and rummaged inside his jacket for the makings as he found a shoe-keg and drew it closer to the forge's pleasant heat. While twisting up his cigarette he watched the blacksmith, then, when he lit up and blew smoke, he shifted his attention to the town, as much of it as he could see from deep inside the shop. 'Didn't see any cattle on my way in,' he said. 'Lots of sign, but no critters.'

'They drive out of here every autumn with the combined gather of the three big outfits that mostly dominate this high country,' explained the smith, heating the shoe at his forge while he pared and trimmed the other front hoof.

'The cows and bulls and leftovers, they take in closer to the home places, which sort of clears the range around town. Good drive this year, and with prices up, when the menfolk return from railhead in a week or two, I expect there'll be money enough circulating around.'

The bay horse offered no opposition, even when the nailing began. The stranger, knowing nothing about the previous history of his horse, decided from this that at least the animal had been shod before. He sat, warm and comfortable in the gloom of the shop and enjoyed his smoke. He hadn't breakfasted; his intention was to eat a stove-cooked meal in a café, but right at the moment he was neither hungry nor in a hurry.

The burly horse-shoer nailed on both front shoes before setting the remaining blanks to heat while he worked at trimming the rear hooves. He was a relaxed, assured, amiable man. The russet beard gave him the appearance of one of those patriachs from biblical times, but when he swore, which he did easily and often, the illusion was shattered. Evidently, he had been blacksmithing in Mandan for many years, and it seemed evident, also, that not many things would trouble him.

He stopped to rest for a while, when both

hind shoes had been beaten to shape on the anvil, and put a dingy old dented coffeepot on the outer bank of the forge. He rinsed two cracked crockery cups in a bucket and handed one to the stranger as he stood gazing up the roadway where the little low wind was raising dust and bringing a taste of cold.

'Run into any bad weather up north?' he asked, turning casually to gaze at the hunched, seated man.

'Just cold,' the stranger replied, and stepped on his cigarette as the smith lifted the coffeepot and leaned to fill their cups.

As though he believed the stranger were a rangerider the shoer said, 'You put off heading south pretty damned late, you know. All the summertime riders been out of this country for over a month. I suppose you'll get clear of the southward pass towards Raton all right, but some years we get early blizzards, and geting caught down a mountain canyon when a couple feet of snow fall in one night has buried a few fellers down there.'

The stranger knew, and arose when his cup was full to step out front and stand looking off where that grey cloud-wall was, beyond the mountains and above them. He had reason to worry. If he could make it down from the high country to the foothill village of Raton, which lay in New Mexico, the rest of the way would be easy; bearing always southward lay Old Mexico. At the border all his anxieties would vanish.

The smith went to work nailing on a hind shoe and called over as he worked. 'What's it look like up there in the north?'

'Storm,' said the stranger, and tasted the bitter black coffee. 'But it doesn't look to be moving very fast.'

'They seldom do,' stated the smith, clinching nails. 'Been my experience on the high meadow, mister, that what you see by day is what you get by night. If there's snow-banners up there you'll want to ride hard once you leave town, and even then I doubt that you'll get clear of the passes in time.' He finished rasping the finished hoof and moved directly to the other rear one, the final one. 'The chances are fair, I'd say, that this'll be just a little storm. Maybe a smart feller would take a room at the boarding-house for tonight, and by morning he'd know; if there's only a couple inches of snow he could push along. But if it's a blizzard, well, then he wouldn't be floundering in some damned avalanche-filled mountain pass, would he?'

It was sound advice. The stranger drank coffee, kept studying the cloud banks, sniffed the metallic scent of the keening, icy wind, and balanced between what he *wished* to do and what he *ought* to do.

His thought had been simply to have the horse shod then hasten ahead. He did not like towns very much, even under other conditions. On the other hand, he surely didn't want to kill the horse and himself in some lonely, frigid canyon where snowfall ahead and behind could doom them both.

He finished the coffee and strolled back to the heat. 'Where is the rooming-house?'

The bearded man looked up with a hind hoof in his lap and gestured with his clinching-hand. 'Yonder up the road across from the saloon. Upstairs over the stage office. The feller who manages for the stage company here in town, owns the building. His name's Abel Spencer. You'll find him in the downstairs office. Two-bits a night for a room with a bed in it. Flopping space for your bedroll out back is a dime, I think.' The smith went back to his nail-clinching and was engrossed with that, until the stranger walked back up front again to lean in the doorway gazing northward in the direction of the saloon, and directly across the roadway, the rooming-house. Then the smith made a slow, thoughtful study of the strangers back, of his wide shoulders, his lean hips, his weathered and worn attire, his silvered spurs and his tied-down walnut-stocked Colt.

When the stranger slowly turned the blacksmith resumed his clinching. When he was finished with that he scooped up a rasp and dressed the hoof all around, clinches and all. He let the foot down easily and turned with a grateful pat on the bay's rump. 'You're a right nice critter to handle,' he told the horse. 'Not every young animal's as nice to be around.' He walked up and ran a hand under the bay's skimpy mane, looked long at the animal's neck, then went on talking and patting the horse. 'You'd take a man a long ways. Damned few good-blooded horses come through this country, son. You've got the breeding all right.' As the smith tossed his tools into the bucket he lugged with him from hoof to hoof, he reached back to untie the shiny old apron. 'Be a dollar,' he said to the stranger. 'That's my going rate; two-bits per hoof.' He raised direct, friendly eyes. 'Fair enough?'

The stranger smiled and walked back, digging with his right hand into a trouser pocket. 'Fair enough, blacksmith. I'm obliged.'

The horse was between them, standing relaxed and hipshot in the pleasant warmth of the glowing forge. When his owner moved around on the left to hand the blacksmith a crumpled

26

dollar note, a long-barrelled dragoon revolver was tipped up towards his face. When the stranger stopped dead in his tracks, the russet-bearded blacksmith's direct, pale eyes showed no trace of their earlier amiability at all.

'It's a bad business, horse-stealing,' the blacksmsith announced very softly. 'Mister, reach across with your left hand and lift out that sixgun and drop it...Mister; I can't keep from blowing a barrel-size hole through your belly from this distance. Now, do like I said.'

The stranger's dark eyes neither blinked nor moved. He stood easy and unmoving. 'What in the hell is wrong with you, blacksmith?'

'Nothing much. Mister; I'm not going to tell you again to shuck the Colt. On the high meadow we hang horse-thieves—but it's also plumb legal to shoot them. You want to get shot, resisting, or do you want to shuck the damned gun and take your chances with the hangrope?'

'It's my horse, blacksmith.'

'Maybe. Suppose we let the marshal figure that out. For the last time—*shed that gun!*'

The stranger obeyed, taking his time to cross over with his left hand to empty the holster on his right hip. Then he looked flintily at the shorter, thicker, older man, his face smoothed out with wariness and wonderment. 'You make mistakes like this often?'

The blacksmith motioned with the long-barrelled cavalry revolver. 'Back up. Back all the way out to the doorway. No, sir, I don't make mistakes like this very often. I never made one like this before, and now isn't going to be the first time. 'You like to know why?'

'Sure would, blacksmith.'

'Did you notice the little brand under this horse's mane, mister? It's three letters—H and R and D. Them first two stand for Hugh Robert and the third letter stands for Deming. Did you know that?'

The stranger hadn't known it. He said nothing.

The blacksmith gestured again. 'Turn now, mister, and walk over next door to the livery-barn. The feller who runs it is also our town marshal, here in Mandan. He happens to be my brother. Edward. Last night he showed me a wire he got from some town up in Wyoming from a sheriff who sent out messages in all directions for a feller who stole a bay part-thoroughbred gelding with the letters HRD branded under his mane on the leftside. Quite a coincidence, isn't it, mister? All right; now let's us just walk next door to the liverybarn office slow and easy-like. Remember—from ten feet behind you I can't help but blow your lights out.'

The stranger appeared to swallow, hard. He did not offer a single word, and when he turned he seemed momentarily unsteady on his feet. Then he walked ahead of the burly, bearded man.

The little low wind had stopped, but the cold seemed to be increasing, and it was very still. Not many people were abroad. That odd metallic scent seemed to hang in the atmosphere. Far northward those billowy big grey-looking clouds were thicker and higher but they still did not seem to have moved from beyond the mountaintops.

CHAPTER 3

The Feel of a Place

Edward Teel did not wear a beard like his brother Hank, the blacksmith, but he had the same colour russet hair, and he was built along the same burly, thick lines. He was a little older than the blacksmith; at least he looked and acted a little older. He escorted the stranger, and his brother, to the stone jailhouse up next to the saloon, which was like an icebox inside and had the musty smell of a place that had been uninhabited a long while. There, he did not say a word until he had made the stranger empty his pockets atop a desk, and had then locked the stranger into the only jail cell Mandan possessed. When all that had been tended to, though, Edward Teel went to light a fire in the iron stove to take the chill off, and while he was doing that he conducted his interrogation. Meanwhile, the bearded blacksmith put the stranger's Colt with his other belongings atop the desk, and sat down to listen.

Marshal Teel wanted to know where the

stranger was from, what his name was, what he had to say about riding a stolen horse, where he was going, and finally, when he turned to gaze past the bars at the prisoner, he asked if the stranger could give him one good reason why the law in Mandan shouldn't hold him on a charge of horse-stealing.

The stranger proved not to be a very talkative man, nor a very informative one. He looked Marshal Teel right in the eye and said his name was John Hampton, that he was originally from Idaho, and that he had met a stranger on the trail up north and had traded with him for the bay horse. To every other question he repeated what he had already said, that he was from Idaho, was named Hampton, and had traded for the horse.

Ed and Hank Teel exchanged a look, then the blacksmith said, 'Describe this feller you traded with for the horse,' and the stranger took his time at making a smoke, at lighting it, and afterwards at quietly gazing over at the blacksmith without saying a word.

Ed the liveryman-marshal threw up his hands. 'I'll go send off a wire to that sheriff up in Wyoming, Hank. He'll maybe have something more.' After the liveryman had left, his brother the blacksmith arose and strolled to the side of the jail cell.

With his amiable look back in place Hank said, 'A feller heading down off the high meadow country to Raton on the desert, would only have to keep travelling south and he'd be in Mexico, wouldn't he, Mister Hampton?'

The prisoner turned his back and went to gaze out the very narrow, barred window in the backwall, where a frosted countryside complete with naked tree-limbs, looked bleak and forbidding.

Hank did not give up. 'Why the hell didn't you steal one with shoes on; that way you wouldn't have had to come to town.'

The stranger kept his back to the blacksmith, kept gazing stonily out across the cold rangeland, westward. When he stomped out his smoke he finally turned and said, 'What did you say your name was, blacksmith?'

'Hank. Henry Teel. What of it; you aim to remember it and come looking for me?' Hank smiled and slowly wagged his head. 'Mister; when my brother gets his wire back from Wyoming, I'm betting you're going to get strung up.' Hank did not act malevolent nor apprehensive. 'Well; however it turns out, you sure shouldn't have come into town.' Hank went over to get the stove damper. 'Have you eaten today, Hampton, or whatever your name is?'

The prisoner hadn't eaten, and now he had no appetite, so he sat on the straw-filled mattress of the wall-bunk without answering, and studied his work-coarsened big hands. What a fool he had been; what a damned, inexcusable, weak-kneed fool. The whole gawddamned scheme was ruined, and by something he had anticipated, had known could happen if he rode into a town, and still, he had ridden into one. What made it so bad was that he had *known* it could happen, and yet he had gone ahead and done it.

There was no way to place the blame elsewhere, so he had to sit there and know a full measure of bitterness. After all the careful planning, a year and more of it, he had done exactly what he had known not to do, because he had heard of other men who had failed miserably and for a year and more he had been adopting, and rejecting, different plans, until he had the perfect one.

And the flaw hadn't arisen from his longing for a woman, as it had with those other men he had heard about, or from exposure or hunger or sickness; he had taken precautions against every one of those things. It had arisen from his feelings for a horse. Not a girl; a gawddamned bay horse.

Hank Tell returned to the outer bars of the

cell, gripped them and said, 'Listen, Hampton, when my brother gets back tell him if you are hungry. I got to get back to the shop.'

The prisoner did not even look up until after Hank Teel had closed the jailhouse door after himself. Then he looked up, and got up, and paced his cage like a bear, ranging a bright, crafty glance everywhere for a means of escape. If he were in the little outer office he could simply have lifted the door-bar and walked out like Hank had done. But he was not in the outer office, and his cell was built to contain anything that was locked inside it. He rattled the door and tested the wall-bolts. He stood on the edge of the bunk and tried with all his strength to get an inch of yield from any of the window-bars, and failed.

By the time the liveryman returned the prisoner was leaning disconsolately upon the back-wall of solid stone, completely convinced no one had ever broken out of his cell, convinced that no one ever would in the future, either.

Marshal Teel went to stand with his back to the crackling little stove. 'Getting almighty cold out,' he told the stranger without a trace of antagonism in his voice. 'You'd never have made it southward down to the desert anyway,' he said. 'We're going to catch it tonight.'

34

The stranger showed interest. 'Snow?'

Ed Teel shook his head. 'Blizzard, mister. Not just snow, a blizzard. I know—it's too early; blizzards don't hit Colorado's high meadow country until maybe mid-October or November, and this is only the first of October. But I'll tell you something I've learned from living here most of my life. Some years winter comes early and comes with a fierce storm, and a man can smell it and feel it a week before it arrives, all the way from Montana to the lower slopes of the New Mexico side.'

The stranger sighed and went back to perch on the edge of the bunk looking out. That little iron stove had heated the entire jailhouse swiftly and very comfortably. But of course the building was not very large, and stone walls as thick as those were made their own insulation.

Ed Teel stepped ahead a few feet, the stove was too hot. He said, 'Have you eaten?'

The dark-eyed man shook his head. 'No. But I lost my appetite between your brother's place and in here. Maybe later.'

Teel sympathized. 'Sure. I don't blame you.' He sauntered to the cell and leaned on the bars. 'You don't wish you'd ridden around this place any more than I also wish you had, Hampton. Especially this time of year.' Ed Teel did not explain what the time of year had to do with

35

it and the prisoner did not ask. 'And if that sheriff up in Wyoming wants you for trial, he's going to have to come get you because we don't have any way to deliver you up there.'

Very few back-range towns had telegraph offices. If the fugitive had used his head, he told himself now, he'd have turned back the moment he entered Mandan and saw that damned cubbyhole office on the east side of the road. Except for that one flaw, that dingy little scruffy office, by now he would be riding southward towards the last mountains to keep him from his eventual destination.

So *gawddamned* near, and now, probably finished, because if they knew he had stolen the bay horse, they had also found the older horse he had abandoned, with its Montana brand, and even a part-time town marshal could not avoid seeing the connection all the way back up to where the southward trail had begun. Up *there* they wouldn't hesitate to come down to Mandan for him, no matter how much snow fell; up there they wouldn't even think of a horse-stealing charge!

Teel leaned and studied his prisoner. What he saw inspired respect; the stranger was heavy-boned, big and flat, weathered and seasoned in all climates. He had the ruddy, faintly coppery look, of maybe a quarter-breed Indian,

36

but the features were good, not coarse. The stranger's eyes were black and steady. He looked exactly like what he probably had been most of his life, a hell of a good all-around rangeman; good at calving, at roping, good with the altering knife, the hot-iron, the glass-backed broncs that tried to half kill a man every morning after breakfast.

Ed Teel said, 'How old are you, Hampton?' The black eyes were guileless. 'Thirty, Marshal. How old are you?'

Teel smiled. 'Thirty-five, but some days I feel fifty. Especially in winter when my joints stay stiff from cold all the damned day long. Bad thing, what riding bad horses does to a man, isn't it? When I was twenty no bump was too hard. Now, I can feel every lousy one over again every time it snows.'

The black eyes remained steadily on Teel. 'That's true, Marshal, and the worst part of it is that as the winters keep passing...' The prisoner shrugged wide shoulders and left the rest of it unsaid.

A middle-sized greying man wearing a gold watch chain across his vest came in from outside and looked first at the prisoner, then at Edward Teel. He had a pinched little slit of a mouth and marble-sized grey eyes that missed nothing. 'Just talked to Hank,' he told Ed

Teel. 'He said you already sent a wire up to Wyoming on this feller.'

Teel nodded. 'He told me his name was John Hampton and that he's from Idaho and that he traded for the thoroughbred horse on the trail.'

'Likely,' sniffed the greying man, shooting a look of dislike at the prisoner. 'Hank says he was fixing to hit me up for a room. I'd have smelt him out if he had, you can bet your money on that.'

Teel crossed to the desk and looked at a paper lying there. 'The description of the horse is good enough, Abel, but we can't hold this feller forever on just that.'

The greying man scowled swiftly. He looked like the kind of person who did everything swiftly, like a bird, or like a lizard. His name was Abel Spencer and he not only owned the rooming-house but also managed the stage-line office in Mandan. 'You can hold him as long as it'll take,' he said, being assertively aggressive. 'I seen that neck-brand and that's more'n enough proof of guilt, Ed. I've leaned on many a rope for fellers convicted for a lot less.'

Teel did not argue, he simply said, 'It's not our job, Abel. I wired to that sheriff up in Wyoming that we got a horse down here

38

answering his description of the stolen one, but someone's got to tie this feller to the theft.'

Abel Spencer glared at the prisoner, then turned his back on the cell and blinked at Teel. 'Sure. If he can't come up with something better than this weak yarn about trading for that horse with some other drifter, he's a goner. And from the looks of him I'd say he's never going to prove anything like that. He's a 'breed, from the looks of him. You know what they are like, Ed. In the past we've had our share of trouble from that kind, around Mandan.'

The town marshal re-read the telegram from Wyoming and let the silence run on and on, until Abel Spencer fidgeted. Finally, when the older man had had enough silence he spoke again, his tone as aggressive as ever, his words as bitingly harsh. 'I think we'd best call a meeting of the Town Council at the saloon tonight, Ed, and hash this over. It's been a long while since we've had a real outlaw in our jailhouse.'

Spencer did not wait for Teel to respond to this suggestion, he turned and stamped out of the office and closed the door loudly after himself. From within the cell the man calling himself Hampton said, 'I've been avoiding that kind all my grown life, but they are everywhere, aren't they?'

Teel was non-committal. 'Spencer talks, is all. And it's just as well most of the cattlemen are gone on the annual drive, otherwise he might stir up something. But how else do folks react to horsethieves?'

'I wasn't thinking about the horsethief part, Marshal. I was thinking about that crack he made about 'breeds, and what he said about leaning on a few hangropes. I know Mister Spencer and I've never seen him before in my life, and like I told you, I've been tring to avoid his kind ever since I was big enough to feel suffocated every time I heard one of them.'

Ed said, 'I'll go get you some stew at the café,' and departed. When he opened and closed the door a blast of frigid air came in from the roadway because the wind was rising again.

CHAPTER 4

A Bad Night, A Worse Morning

Darkness came early and not even the massive stone walls could entirely deaden the sound of a savage wind. When Ed Teel brought his prisoner a pan of stew and a slice of limp pie, he lit the lamp and set it on the far side of the door so that it wouldn't be blown out every time someone let in a blast of wind. He also banked the iron stove with oak knots that would burn like coal and, hopefully, last the full night long. When he had done all that, had slid the food under the cell door, he said, 'I'll tell you something, stranger: If you'd left town this morning after Hank shod your horse—*somebody's* horse—by now you'd be almost to the edge of the southward pass with no chance to go on and no chance to turn back. So, maybe what's happened is for the best.'

The prisoner leaned on the bars looking out at Teel, ignoring the food at his feet. 'I'd rather have taken my chances on the trail,' he said. 'There are worse things than freezing to death.'

Teel was at the stove checking it, and looked up slowly. 'You did steal that bay horse, didn't you?'

The black-eyed man gave Teel look for look through a moment of long silence, then he bent, picked up the stew and went back to sit on the edge of the bunk and start eating.

Ed was wearing a sheep-pelt lined coat that hampered his movements but which would keep out just about any kind of cold. He watched his prisoner eat, and the full knowledge arrived about this stranger: They might hang him back in Wyoming, or something might happen to him in Mandan, but he would never say a word he did not want to say freely, no matter what kind of coaxing or what kind of force, was used to make him do otherwise. Teel's attention was diverted by a powerful wind-blast against the front of the building. A second blast struck from the north and the lamplight flickered from draught.

'It'll stop after a bit,' he said to the prisoner, although what he actually was doing was thinking aloud. 'And it'll get as quiet as the inside of a grave—and the snow will come.'

The prisoner looked out. 'You're sure, are you?'

Teel nodded. 'Plumb sure. It'll be a bad one too. Well; I figure you're all right until morning.' He balanced there, waiting, and when the prisoner ignored him, Ed left his jailhouse. The prisoner cocked his head at the sound of a heavy lock being swung into place between two outside hasps. Whatever else happened in Mandan this night, the prisoner was not going to know until morning.

He finished eating and toed the stewpan back under the door. Then he made a cigarette, lay back his full length on the wall-bunk and listened to the wild night.

Teel was probably right; if he had ridden southward, by now he would be nearing the mountain pass. By nine or ten o'clock he would be riding down in through the freezing wind and the total darkness—and maybe by twelve or one o'clock the snow would have caught him down there.

But the alternative was no more cheerful. They wouldn't hang him in Wyoming over the bay horse, because some enterprising lawman would back-track him all the way. They would hang him in Montana.

The lamp flickered every time a frigid blast battered the jailhouse walls, then, after a while, exactly as Marshal Teel had predicted, the wind died to a whisper, and eventually died away altogether.

The man calling himself John Hampton arose

43

and paced like a caged cougar. Eventually he leaned at the barred window, but there was nothing to be seen out there but stygian blackness; no stars, no lights up or down the alleyway, no signs of life of any kind. He had a sensation of being helpless, of being trapped. It was a new feeling. All his life he had been free. He had faced nature's worst almost ever year. Sometimes he had suffered for it, sometimes he had come through without suffering, too, but this was the first time he could ever remember feeling totally helpless and incapable of protecting himself. He thought of the bay horse, but at least he did not realize he was also in detention, at the liverybarn, so he was probably eating a flake of hay in a draughty stall, perfectly content.

There was no other living thing to think about. The black-eyed man had nothing else— unless it was his saddlebats lashed high in an aspen tree a mile or two from Mandan. He did not worry about them. If it snowed during the night no one would ever know he had been up there in that aspen grove.

But if they took him back to Wyoming…if they hanged him up there…?

There had to be a way out. Always before when he'd been in bad situations there had been a way out. But those other times he had not been locked in, which was the difference.

He examined his cell again, but more minutely this time; it still came out the same. Probably, the town marshall's blacksmithing brother had manufactured the steel cage. Hank was the resourceful, ingenious type; when he did a job he would do it exactly right. If an escape could be made, it would have to be accomplished some other way, because no one could break out of this steel cage.

Gradually, the darkness outside seemed to softly brighten, seemed to be assuming a ghostly opaqueness. It was snowing. The prisoner arose to peer out the window. The flakes were beautiful. As large almost as a man's palm, and drifting downwards without haste, and building up with a lovely soft silence that shut out every sound, making the world beyond the cell window close in, closer and closer until they appeared to insulate the man looking at them, at their downy accumulation, against everything in the world beyond the immediate scope of his alleyway view.

An hour later Marshal Teel returned. His hat and shoulders were white and his breath steamed in the warm jailhouse. As he knocked snow from his hat against one leg, he looked at the lamp's reservoir of coal-oil, then checked the glowing oak knots in the stove. 'You'll be all right until morning,' he told the prisoner. 'By then we're going to have a couple of feet of snow all over the high meadow. I told you.'

The prisoner said, 'Bad night for travellers.'

'Like I told you,' agreed the liveryman, 'if you'd been on the trail, by now you'd be in trouble. By morning you'd be stiff as a ramrod.'

The black-eyed man looked scornful. 'Haven't you ever been through a snowfall before?'

Teel said, 'Sure. Mark my words, Hampton, this isn't just a snowfall.' Then Teel changed the topic. 'We had a meeting at the saloon a little while ago, about you. If the weather gets too bad won't anybody from Wyoming be able to get down here for you. The Town Council voted to hold your trial here.'

The prisoner said, 'You got a judge in Mandan?'

'Yeah. You met him today, Abel Spencer. He is also the mayor and President of the Town Council.'

The prisoner's wide mouth parted in a white-toothed smile. 'Shoot me right now, Marshal. Save the oak knots and the coal-oil.'

Teel looked over at the crackling stove, then turned towards the desk. He stood over there a moment pawing through the prisoner's effects. 'What's your real name, Hampton?'

The prisoner kept smiling. 'John Smith.'
Teel looked up. 'John Smith, horsethief?'
'No. John Smith lynch-law victim, Marshal.
Unless you'll get this silly thing over with
sooner. Tell them I tried to escape. Spencer will
believe it. If I was manacled and leg-chained
and you shot me inside the cell, he'd believe
I was trying to escape.'

Teel dropped down in the desk-chair, folded
his hands in front of his face and gazed for a
long time at his prisoner. 'There's not going
to be a lynching,' he said, so softly the stranger
had to bend to hear. 'I reckon you're a horsethief, mister. I don't doubt that at all. And I've
lost horses to nightriders out of my pasture west
of town. If I'd caught them at it I'd have done
my level best to kill them on the spot.'

The prisoner said, 'Gun or rope?'

'Either way,' replied Teel. 'Gun if I could,
rope if I had to.'

The prisoner's forehead furrowed. 'And
me...?'

Teel threw himself back in the chair and
loosened the sheep-pelt coat. 'Four years ago,
before I was town marshal, the feller who held
the job—he's out of the country now—he and
some other fellers strung up a cow-thieving
homesteader from western Colorado. He had
the green hides in his old wagon with the

47

brands still on them.'

'And?'

'Like you, mister, he said he bought the hides on the trail. It was the truth—but he'd been dead four months before folks had the proof shoved in their faces.' Teel let the quiet stretch out before continuing to speak. 'Not me. I really believe you stole that bay horse. But I'll tell you something, Hampton; in thirty-five years I've been wrong maybe five hundred times. Only it didn't much matter about those things, they weren't like killing the wrong man would be.' Teel rocked forward. 'So, there's not going to be a lynching.' He stood up. 'If that sheriff from Wyoming will get down here and take you off our hands, that'll solve a lot of things.' Teel began buttoning his coat as he moved towards the door from behind the desk. 'Only he's not going to make it. Not now, and my guess would be that he won't be able to make it for maybe two, three weeks. I may be a lousy town marshal, like I've heard it rumoured some folks think, but I know the weather in this country.'

Teel reached the door, cast a final look around, then said, 'I'll fetch along some breakfast in the morning. Good night.'

The black-eyed man neither spoke nor nodded as he watched the liveryman depart. He listened to the same sounds of a heavy lock being forced into place through door-hasps, and turned, eventually, to go stand by the alley window looking out.

Now, the world was no longer black anywhere he could see, but the whiteness was just as bad because it concealed things, hid them under mounds and soft piles and drifts that had whirls and cuves to them as they grew steadily larger.

Sure enough, if he and the bay horse had ridden southward by now they would be trying desperately to keep snow trampled inside a little circle praying they could keep moving until morning and praying even harder that the snow would stop by morning. In all probability they would have died out there just exactly as the liveryman had said.

Eventually, unable to do anything else, the prisoner returned to the bunk and stretched out full length. He did not intend to sleep, but he did. The jailhouse was warm, he had been days and nights in the cold until his muscles had become almost permanently bunched into knots. Until he'd sat by Hank Teel's glowing forge earlier in the day, he hadn't sat by anything better than a cooking fire in a long while.

He slept so soundly morning arrived and he

still slept, something he had rarely done before in his life. By nature he was an early riser. Men who matured in bunkhouses and cow-camps, got that way just naturally. By the time the sun came, they had already fed their stock, shaved, washed, rolled their bedding and had at least one cup of coffee at the cook's fire.

When he opened his eyes, eventually, the jailhouse had an increasingly steady chill creeping in through the stone walls. The stove still gave off heat, but from oak-ash, not from fire.

Inside, the whole building was frosty-pale, like an icehouse was when a man entered without a candle or a lantern. He arose, scratched, then went to the alley window and gazed out.

It was still snowing. The flakes had neither decreased in size nor hastened in their downfall, but all night long they had not slackened even once, with a result that made the prisoner let his breath out in a long sigh. The liveryman had been right; if he and the bay horse had been down-country, even if they'd managed to tramp all night to stay atop the buildup, they would be doomed because by now they would be staggering blind and stumbling, and the snow still kept coming. They would have died.

Nothing seemed able to stop that kind of snowfall, neither warmth nor wind nor even a sleety rainfall. The prisoner made his first smoke of the day and watched until he heard someone hit the front door with a heavy shoulder, heard them knocking the snow-choked big lock against its hasps to free the keyhole. He turned towards the outer office and waited.

When Ed Teel came in he had remnants of clinging snow higher than his knees. He was bundled in a woollen scarf and had his hat pull-ed down almost to his ears. He shook like a dog coming out of a creek, then went at once to build up the fire in the stove. While he was do-ing that he said, 'Glad to see you didn't freeze. It's bad out there and I don't see any sign of it letting up.' Then he finished at the stove and walked thoughtfully to the front of the cell. 'And it happened like it happens every damned blizzard—last night ice build-up broke the telegraph wires.' He returned his prisoner's stare. 'That's what I meant yesterday when I said you had to come along this time of year.'

The prisoner didn't understand. 'Well...?'

Teel pulled off his blanket-lined rider's gloves. 'Hampton, with those wire down I'm not going to get an answer from that Wyoming sheriff. Not about you and not about the bay horse. Remember what I told you last night?'

The prisoner had a glimmer. 'They'll try me

51

here; that stage-company manager with the rat-trap mouth will be the judge?'

Marshal Teel woodenly inclined his head.

CHAPTER 5

The Aftermath

The snow did not stop falling until shortly after noon. By then it was more than two feet deep. But in the stillness the day got warmer; snow was insulation.

Mandan huddled under a leaden sky, and where people worried about ceiling rafters men climbed aloft and shovelled the build-up off their roofs. People also made little trails, and merchants, with little or no business, spent some of their time pushing snow off the plank-walks out front. Gradually, the snowed-in town began to reassume a look of life. Even the roadway became rutted when a few rigs and a couple of cutters with broad runners, ploughed back and forth.

But Mandan's activity was limited. Pathways led to wood sheds, to the front walk, to the general store and back again. There were drifts up the north walls of almost every building, and where heat from inside had melted the under-layer of roof-snow, great slides had rumbled from rooftops to meet the drifts, making the walls of some buildings completely covered from the ground to the eaves.

Commerce was practically at a standstill. All morning men concentrated on digging out, and when that had been accomplished, they had time on their hands. Ed Teel, for example, helped his day hostler clear both front and back doorways to his liverybarn, helped take some of the horses out back to the corrals, breaking trail with the first four or five, but after that there was little to do, unless a man wanted to make work, so Ed tramped next door to his brother's shop. There, Hank had his *forge* going, but for heat not because he had any blacksmithing to do. Hank poured a cup of black coffee for Ed and stood morosely with his back to the forge looking out into the white-mounded roadway.

'It'll melt in a few days,' he said to Ed, without sounding too hopeful. 'The first storm never hangs on.'

Ed swished coffee and kept his thoughts to himself. It wasn't going to melt, first storm or not, and unless Ed's deduction was dead wrong, there would be more storm. He changed the subject by relating for Hank's benefit the results of the Town Council's meeting at the saloon the previous night. Hank listened

54

without taking his eyes off the big drifts yonder. Then he turned to tromp the forge treadle which made the fire brisk up with little cracklings. 'I don't know much law,' he told Ed, 'but it don't sound right, trying a man in Colorado for something he did in Wyoming. I always thought that was why outlaws ran for it—so's they'd be out of reach of the law back where they committed the crime.'

'Outlaws run,' stated Ed, 'because they don't want to get caught. Hampton, or whatever his name is, can be tried here; it's called a change of venue.'

'Don't you have to have the permission of the Wyoming authorities, or something like that, Ed?'

The town marshal drained his coffee cup before answering. 'Lot of things we ought to have,' he conceded, 'but aren't going to get, now that the telegraph wires are down, and the snow's too deep for someone to back-track and find the break.' He set the cup aside and moved closer to the forge. 'It's Spencer's idea. You know how he is about outlaws. I reckon he's that way from so many years of serving the stage company. Nobody gets robbed as often as stage-line people.'

Hank began to lose interest in the forthcoming trial. 'How's Hampton feel about it?'

Remembering the prisoner's comment that Ed should shoot him now and save the expense of delay, Ed shook his head. 'Not real happy.'

Hank drew up a shoe-keg and sat beside his forge. 'You know, on days like this with nothing to do, a man gets to thinking, Ed. I was making up my mind about something when you walked in just now.'

'What's that?'

The blacksmith stared out into the wintry day again as he answered. 'The best way to deal with horsethieves is do it right on the spot, when you catch them. That way it's over and done with, folks get back to work, and no one knows the thief as anything but an outlaw that they got no use for... But Hampton's still around, and I remember how he looked at me yesterday, before I drew on him, and how we talked easy-like about the weather and horses and other stuff. You know, Ed: like we'd maybe ridden together or something. He was able to smile and joke a little and hell, it's different hanging a man you feel that you know that well.'

Ed watched his brother's bearded face. 'What was the thing you made up your mind about?'

Hank did not meet Ed's gaze when he replied. 'I'll never do that again. Horsethief or not, that is the law's job. I might even let the next one ride on, even if I know, like I did yesterday.' Finally, Hank raised his solemn eyes. 'And I don't figure it's right, trying him there for whatever he done in Wyoming. I figure that's more of Abel Spencer's vindictiveness, not the real law.'

Ed smiled at his brother. 'Once in a long while you make sense,' he said, enigmatically, and walked out of the shop heading for the café with the steamy window and the woodsmoke-smell where he had his breakfast and got a pan of the same assortment for his prisoner. As he was leaving he told the grumpy old caféman he ought to clean his flue and haul his ashes so the stove would draw better and not smoke so much. After Ed had departed the indignant caféman called him a very unflattering name.

The jailhouse was as warm as toast, still, and Teel's prisoner had regained his appetite. The fact that he had over-slept did not seem relevant; an early-riser in a jail cell with no place to go and nothing to do, could only spend that many more tortuous hours.

But the prisoner had been thinking, which was about all he could do without restrictions, and as he ate he told Ed his understanding of the law was that unless a prisoner was charged, he could not be held in jail.

57

Ed knew a little more law than that, so he explained that a prisoner could he held until he either posted bail or until maybe a week or something like that had passed which was the limit a prisoner could be held incommunicado. Actually, although Ed had read a law book inherited from his predecessor as town marshal, some of it he did not believe, some of it had put him to sleep, and some of it he did not quite understand. In matters of procedure and detail, Ed usually deferred to Abel Spencer, who had three law books.

Last night, during the storm, Abel had made it plain that Hampton would not be admitted to bail. Ed had wondered about that, but Abel had also said that, as legal representative of the township's judicial district, it was his prerogative to interpret the law as he saw fit. 'No bail for that damned horsethief!'

Ed did not relay this wording to the prisoner. He simply said he could hold Hampton for maybe as long as a week. Then he shrugged and said, 'Where would you go if I turned you out?' meaning that Mandan was snow bound in all directions, which was the truth, and which seemed likely to remain the truth for some time yet to come.

The prisoner ate and thought about that. Another time he would have been quite content. He did not have to haul water or wood, he had his meals brought to him, he could sleep as long as he wished, and whenever he wished, and none of this cost him a copper penny.

But it was still restriction. To someone less accustomed than the black-eyed prisoner to being completely free, to being able to look far out, for miles, and see only rangeland and mountains and forests, four walls set close in may not have been as stifling as it was to Hampton. But that other, mythical person, was not in the Mandan jailhouse, Hampton was. He finished eating, pushed the tin back under the steel-barred door and stood up to stretch and go peer out his rearwall window for the hundredth time.

'This is the second day,' he said to Ed Teel, without looking away from the snowscape out yonder. 'Three more and you set me loose.' Now, he finally turned.

Teel's problem was that he knew the telegraph line could not be mended within three days, and without verification from the sheriff up in Wyoming, which he had been waiting for when the blizzard had struck, the prisoner was correct, Teel would be obliged to set Hampton free.

'We'll see,' he said evasively, and the prisoner stood looking out at him.

'If you don't,' said Hampton, 'you'll be up in it with me to your hocks, Marshal.'

Ed was not cowed. 'Relax. Like I said what good would it do, you being out there in the cold? You can't get a hundred yards from town for snow, and there's more coming.'

The prisoner was not ameliorated. 'I could go up to the saloon and maybe play cards. Or I could stand out front of the store and watch folks stare at me. Or maybe I could just sit across the desk from you, out there, and beat you at checkers... When will they have that telegraph line fixed?'

Teel was not fooled. His prisoner, too, realized how vitally important that line was to him. Every now and then Hampton would reveal, always by implication, his secret fear. That was enough to convince Ed he had a genuine felon on his hands.

'Hard to say,' replied the liveryman-marshal. 'If the line busted close in, maybe a couple of fellers could snowshoe their way out and repair it.'

Hampton's strong face turned sardonic. 'Yeah. And if it's busted five miles out?'

Teel said, 'Providing no more snow falls, that would take a little longer. Listen, Hampton, be content where you are. Believe me, it's the best place to be right now.'

The prisoner slowly shook his head. 'No sir. Even freezing in a snowbank is better than being caged like an animal, and you know it.'

Hampton crossed his cell to the front wall and stood that much closer to the man at the battered old desk in the outer office. Steady blue eyes regarded him from beyond the bars. Teel had treated Hampton well, had explained things to him he hadn't had to explain, had talked to him without noticeable rancour or antagonism. As an individual, Hampton could like Ed Teel, but it was next to impossible to view Ed Teel as just another saddlehorseman as long as he sat out there at his lawman's desk while Hampton had the steel bars to grip with both hands and stare out through.

Teel finally leaned, opened a drawer and ploughed through some useless contents and straightened back up holding aloft a folded board. 'Checkers?'

Hampton shrugged. 'You can't beat me. I've spent too many days like this in bunkhouses playing some of the best men who ever set up a checkerboard.'

Teel smiled and dragged over a chair and a little bench. He set the bench next to the bars where Hampton could reach through, and Hampton drew the solitary chair inside his cell up close, on the opposite side of the bars. Teel

61

did not take the customary precaution of leaving his holstered sixgun on the desk before sitting down. He was not the least bit apprehensive; as he had already pointed out, even if the prisoner got out of his cell, there just was no place for him to go.

As they played Hampton said, 'How come this Abel Spencer has the right to try me for something that didn't even happen in this state?'

Teel explained that about as he'd explained it to his brother at the blacksmith shop. Hampton listened, concentrated on their game for a while, then said, 'Marshal, it's beginning to look to me like you are in a worse position than I'm in.'

Teel looked up. 'What do you mean?'

Hampton jumped three of Teel's men, and grinned out through the bars. 'You said last night there would be no lynching. Spencer is going to hand me sure as he's a foot high, and he's going to do it out of prejudice and nothing else. None of you can prove I stole that bay horse. There's just no way for you to prove it with the telegraph line busted and you know that's true. But that bastard is going to hang me—and that's lynching pure and simple, isn't it?'

This was of course Teel's problem, put succinctly. He hadn't quite faced it yet, not this bluntly anyway, but there it was. One reason why he'd chosen not to face it yet was because he hadn't had to, wouldn't have to face it in fact, until he had to either release the prisoner or escort him up to the backroom at the stage-line office where court was held. Another reason he could procrastinate was because the blizzard had disrupted everything, including Abel Spencer's stage schedules, and that kept Abel diverted.

Teel frowned over the loss of his three checkers and concentrated on the game without answering Hampton—or whatever his name was.

But he still got beaten. Not just once, but five out of six games, before the early dusk closed in and they stopped playing.

CHAPTER 6

The Judge's Dictum

The next day it warmed up considerably and people took heart from this, even as they cursed the runoff that choked gutters and cut ruts out in the centre of the road.

Three stranded travellers kept vigil with Abel Spencer at the stage-line office hoping the northward coach would make it through to Mandan on its southward run. It did not arrive by mid-morning, and as Ed Teel told Hampton over their fresh checker game, it wasn't going to arrive.

'Just because we got a nickel's worth of a chinook wind don't mean the roads are open again. And you remember what I'm telling you: one of these sudden warm spells only means there's warm air being pushed down out of the north ahead of another big cold front.'

Hampton laughed and shook his head. 'You'd ought to trade that badge for a weather prophet's wand.' Then Hampton went ahead and beat Ed Teel three checker games in a row and although Teel was a good loser, this was piling it up on him a little strong, so he quit and went to make them a pot of coffee.

Hampton leaned back on the chair inside his cell and said, 'Two more days after this one, Ed, and I'm curious about something.'

Teel continued to work at the stove as he said, 'What about?'

'Just how good your word is.'

Teel looked over his shoulder and saw Hampton's black eyes shining with hard humour. Ed said, 'You like this, don't you? You're gettin' a big kick out of putting me on the spot between you and Abe Spencer.'

Hampton nodded. 'Misery likes company.'

Teel went back to work with the coffee pot. 'My word's good enough.'

Hank walked in, in shirtsleeves and without his hat. He nodded at the prisoner then watched his brother at the stove as he stepped to a chair and sat down. 'It's sure melting fast now.' Hank was patently very pleased. 'Give it another couple of days, we'll be able to see the ground again.'

'Not if another storm hits,' said his brother, and Hank's cheery expression flattened.

'You always was a gloomy cuss, Ed, but even if it snowed again we've had enough run-off so's a fresh layer wouldn't hurt us too much.'

Ed did not argue. He and Hampton were perfectly willing to leave the initiative with Mother Nature. Ed told his brother there probably wasn't a soul on the high meadow who could beat the prisoner at checkers, and Hank was properly impressed. When Hampton offered him a game, Hank declined.

'No thanks. I got to sashay out to my horse pasture and see how the stock's doing. The old animals will know how to paw down to dead grass. It's the young stock I worry about.' Hank arose and went to the door, then he looked from Hampton to his brother and said, 'I heard a rumour over at the store about Abel fixing to hold court in the morning.'

In the silence that ensued, Hank departed, and outside a watery, thin streak of sunshine broke through the grey overcast to heighten the general impression that the blizzard had come and gone, and perhaps now an Indian summer might follow, allowing everyone perhaps as much as another two weeks or so to get ready for winter.

That sunshine made a soft reflection inside the jailhouse that went unheeded. The prisoner arose from his chair and said, 'Well; I reckon he figured it close, didn't he? Or did you tell him you'd have to set me loose, so he would convene his court first?'

66

Ed had not discussed the date of a trial with Spencer since the meeting up at the saloon. Even then, no one had been specific because no one knew at that time the extent of the damage to the telegraph lines; it had still been thought likely a wire would arrive at Mandan informing Teel that the Wyoming sheriff was on his way, which was how everyone had seemed to want this trouble to end. Except maybe Abel Spencer, whose frustrations and exasperations over the years resulting from stage hold-ups had instilled in him an implacable antipathy towards lawbreakers of any and all kinds.

Hampton was still awaiting his answer when Ed filled two cups at the stove and crossed to silently hand one through the bars. Only then did Teel answer. 'If you figure I cooked this up to get off the hook about releasing you, you're wrong.'

Hampton growled an answer to that. 'Sure almighty convenient, though, isn't it, him trying me one day before you were to set me loose?'

Teel tasted the coffee and although it really was not bad, he had lost his taste for it by now. He turned when someone lifted the outside latch and pushed on the weather-warper door until it yielded. Abel Spencer in a bearskin coat and stiff-brim, flat-crowned freighter's hat, stomped in out of the soggy snow. His quick eyes at once saw the coffee cups. 'Looks just right,' he said, tugging off gloves that hung from a long thong around his neck. 'Ain't much of a coffee-drinker except in weather like this.' Spencer's marble-eyes sprang across to Hampton and remained there. 'Looks like he's getting fat on free food, Edward. Looks like he's getting soft and sassy, sitting around in the warmth while decent people got to work to pay for his keep in here. Well...that's what I came by for. I reckon we'd best hold his hearing right after breakfast in the morning.' Spencer went over where Teel held a full cup extended towards him. 'Thanks, it sure smells good.' Spencer kept gazing into the cup and not meeting Teel's stare as he continued to speak on his original theme. 'Fetch him down to my building after he's eaten, Ed. Keep him chained; I know a vicious man when I see one.'

Hampton felt the futility deep down, but that did not keep him from trying, so he said, 'You got proof, Judge? Maybe the horse is going to testify against me. How the hell can you try a man for a crime that wasn't even committed in your state; a crime you can't possibly prove was even committed?'

Spencer's dry little round eyes flamed with hatred. 'You shut up, whatever-your-name-is.

68

We got the horse. We got the telegram giving particulars about him proving he's the right critter and that he was stolen, and we got the man who hasn't even denied riding him into town. Now just what the hell more do we need?'

Hampton gripped the steel bars until his knuckles whitened. 'You need proof. I know that much, Spencer. You got to prove I didn't trade for the horse on the trail like I said I did.'

Spencer continued to stare viciously at the prisoner. He curled his little pinched mouth in an expression of total contempt. 'We don't have to prove nothing of the sort, you thieving bastard. You *did* it. You can deny that until your last lousy breath if you want to, but you *did* it, and so help me Lord I'm going to see you in hell for that. You're going to be an example folks'll remember forever, that crime don't pay anywhere near Mandan.'

'It didn't happen near Mandan,' exclaimed the prisoner, but Abel Spencer was already on his way out of the jailhouse. He reminded Ed Teel to be sure and arrive promptly after breakfast the following morning, and that was all. Afterwards, Hampton and Teel were left in a solid silence that was thick enough to cut with a knife.

Teel brought the pot over and said, 'Hold out your cup and I'll refill it.'

Hampton's face twisted with a wild expression of fury, only momentarily though, then it smoothed out and he pushed forth the cup with a hand that did not shake. When he pulled back the cull cup he said, 'Thanks,' in a toneless voice, and sank down upon the chair at his back.

Teel stood gazing at his prisoner for a moment, a man with words dammed behind his teeth. He turned, gaining a little time by going over and replacing the coffee pot atop the stove.

The prisoner's voice hit Teel in the back. 'You're going to be part of *that?*'

Teel's nerves were raw; had been raw for a couple of days now. He snapped back. 'Why didn't you *buy* a lousy horse?'

Hampton jutted his chin towards the desk. 'You find enough money in my pockets to pay for a horse?'

Teel sighed; Hampton had given another clear implication of, not only that he had stolen the horse, but why he had stolen it. Teel did not say it, but he was thinking that if Hampton made a remark or two like that tomorrow, Abe Spencer would pick them up instantly. Spencer had a sharp, hard, incisive mind. He

70

would not only see that Hampton was guilty by implication, Abe would also use that very fact against Hampton.

Ed Teel's problem was that he was just as convinced of Hampton's guilt as Abel Spencer was, but for better reasons, but he hung back over a judge pre-judging, and Abe had said it right there in the jailhouse: He was going to see Hampton in hell and make an example of him, and *that*, by gawd, was lynching a man just the same as though there had been no judge and no trial. Hampton had called it that and Hampton had been dead right. Pre-judging and pre-condemnation to death by hanging was lynching no matter what Abel Spencer called it.

Hampton said, 'Come on, set up the checkerboard, Ed. What the hell; if a man can't win in life let him win a little in make-believe.'

Teel had no desire whatsoever to play checkers, and the fore-knowledge that he was going to be beaten had nothing to do with it; he just did not want to play at anything, checkers or anything else, right now.

But he did play. Hank arrived after the first game and drew up a chair to watch Hampton's moves. Then Hank left without a word, and when he arrived again about a quarter hour later, he had a quart of rye whisky and three water glasses.

There was a town rule against liquour inside the jailhouse. Every town had such an ordinance; it prevented hate-filled lawmen from shooting corralled renegades and murderers. Hank poured, and passed out two glasses, Hampton smiled his appreciation and Ed looked at his brother sombrely and said, 'Thanks.' That was all the attention the town rule got.

The play was mostly silent. Men did not speak when they were concentrating. Hank rolled his eyes once, over a move by his brother, but he kept whatever had bothered him to himself. Only after the game was concluded and Hampton, no longer able to derive satisfaction from beating a man he had beaten so often, finished his whisky, did Hank say what had brought him in the first place.

'Your day-man picked up a stray horse out back by the corrals, Ed. He didn't have any bridle but there was a saddle on his back. We figured someone tied the critter by the reins, somewhere, and the horse set back and busted the bridle and run off.'

Hampton kept gazing out at Hank. Hampton, the lifelong rangeman, was puzzled about something. 'Blacksmith, where, around here, would a man be riding in a couple of feet of snow? You didn't by any chance backtrack that horse, did you?'

Hank hadn't. He had told his brother's hostler to off-saddle the horse, stall him and pitch him in some feed because the horse had acted tucked up and about to collapse.

Hampton arose and leaned on the bars looking at Ed. 'No horse would be that bad off just from wandering through this snow from end of town to the other end. Without seeing the horse, I'd guess he come one hell of a long ways, and if he had a rider, maybe, Marshal, you got a hurt man lying out somewhere fixing to freeze to death unless folks find him quick and fetch him in by a fire.'

Ed stood, listening, then he reached for his sheep-pelt coat and hat, jerked his head at his brother and stamped out of the jailhouse in a hurry. Hank left too, and he left so fast, right behind his brother, he did not even have time to look chagrined over his casual blunder.

Hampton made a cigarette, lit it and went to stand by his alley window. The sun was fading now, the sky was darkening again, very early in the afternoon,and that damned liveryman-town-marshal was the most uncanny weather prophet the black-eyed prisoner had ever seen; sure as God made green grass it was going to storm again, and tonight, like Ed Teel had predicted.

Hampton blew smoke and studied the wintery world and wondered whether the weather was for him or against him. If it would hold off and allow someone to repair those telegraph lines, a message might come through from Wyoming that would save him for at least another week. On the other hand, it was possible that by now Wyoming's authorities had back-tracked him to Montana, and if they had, then he might just as well be tried in Colorado.

He smiled bitterly. He had been over a year perfecting the ideal crime, and here he was, in jail. Maybe there was no such thing as a perfect crime.

CHAPTER 7

A Kind of Freedom for Hampton

Marshal Teel did not return to the jailhouse until late evening and by then it had been dark for two hours and that pleasant, day-long warmth, had gradually yielded to an increasing cold.

The prisoner was hungry. He was also out of tobacco. He had all but forgotten the stray horse because of those other, more personal, things, so, when Ed arrived with supper for Hampton, the prisoner asked him to take some of the coins he'd been forced to leave on the desk and buy him a sack of tobacco. Ed departed without a word, to comply, and only after Hampton had sat down to eat did he reflect upon the other man's tight expression and wordlessness.

When Ed returned Hampton was half finished with his meal. He accepted the little tobacco sack through the bars and said, 'Thanks. What's bothering you?'

Teel was short. 'Just finish your supper so's

I can lock this place up for the night.' Ed went to re-fill the bowl of the coal-oil lamp from a tin kept in a cupboard, then he re-lit the lamp and turned next to banking the stove with more oak knots.

Hampton did as he had been ordered, pushed the tin plate under the door with his boot-toe, and went to work making his after-supper smoke. 'Did you back-track that loose horse?' he asked, lighting up and gazing over where Ed was working at the stove.

'For a ways,' Teel replied.

'Which direction?'

'North, up the stage road.'

Hampton scowled. This was like pulling teeth. 'Well?'

Teel clanged the cast-iron stovedoor closed and heaved a big sigh. 'No telling how far that damned horse came, but it was more than a mile and a half, which was as far as Hank and I could make it on horseback.' Teel turned and met Hampton's steady gaze. 'It's getting ready to storm again.' As though that closed the subject Ed shook his head and looked away, but Hampton did not allow the topic to die.

'Well?'

'Hank's harnessing a team to his cutter, but if that feller's very far out it'll start snowing before we get very far. It's about all a horse can do, going a mile out there. The drifts are four feet high in some places on the damned road.'

Hampton scowled. 'You going to let him die out there?'

Ed flared up. He had had a strenuous day. 'No, damn it all. Not if we can help it. But we can't work a miracle, can we?'

Hampton continued to stand and smoke and look out through the bars. 'You got snowshoes? Two men can mush ahead and break trail for a team.'

'And who the hell is going to drive the team if Hank and I mush ahead?'

Hampton said. 'Try Mister Spencer. He's so quick to set things right, let him go along and—'

'He's got his own troubles at the corral yard. He's got three men working for him just shovelling the damned snow away from his haystack to his stage horses.'

'You already asked him?'

Ed nodded. 'Him, and others. Folks know by now we're going to catch it again tonight and they're getting ready. Anyway, maybe the man who owned that horse is already frozen to death. If he isn't, it's still expecting a hell of a lot from someone to maybe meet the same fate trying to find him in a night as pitch black as this one.'

Hampton put out his cigarette and said. 'Try me, Ed. Ask me to help out.'

They looked at one another. Teel turned towards the stove when it popped, then looked back. Hampton read the indecision and said, 'Listen, Ed; I came down that road a few days back, and there are no trees alongside it.'

Teel frowned. 'What of it?'

'That horse wasn't tied and set back to bust his bridle, because there was no place for him to be tied to. You know how that looks to me? Like whoever was riding him took off the bridle and started the horse towards town hoping maybe the horse would make it; hoping someone would come back and find the man.'

Ed Teel turned this over in his mind.

Hampton pushed home another point. 'Ed, you've said it yourself: Where would I go if I was free? If a man on horseback can't get more than a mile or such a matter, how far could I get, on foot, with you and your brother watching me and armed? Open the damned door and loan me a coat and some gloves.'

Teel wavered. 'It's darker than hell out there, Hampton. Another storm is almost overhead. The chances of finding that feller are about the same as for a snowball in hell.'

'But you've got to try,' exclaimed the prisoner. 'I know. I've been through this before, and you can't just let a man die.

Hank came stamping in from out in the icy night. He had a shawl tied over his head under his hat and was wearing an old blanket-coat with bearskin gauntlets. He did not even nod at the prisoner as he said with noticeable impatience, 'Damn it, Ed, you said you'd be right along. Let's shake a leg, or else forget it.'

Ed buttoned his sheep-pelt coat and re-settled the hat atop his head. 'Hampton volunteered to go along.'

Hank looked quickly into the cell, and answered without a moment's hesitation. 'All right, let him out. He'll need a coat and gloves. I got an extra set of snowshoes in the cutter. Well, damn it all, you said it yourself; we got to have another man or it's no use.'

Ed voiced his last objection. 'Abe'll have a fit and he won't be the only one around town.'

Hank was only concerned with the time they were wasting. 'Listen, damn it all, while you're having trouble with your conscience those clouds are getting lower and thicker. Ed; spit or close the window. I'm not wild about breaking a leg out there or getting buried in a blizzard, so whatever you decide, do it *now!*'

Hampton offered his final argument. 'You have my word. I'll stay with you going out and coming back.'

Ed stepped swiftly to his desk, got the cell-door key and went bleakly over and opened the cell. He then flung the key inside on the bunk and whirled towards a cupboard where he dug out a blanket-coat like his brother was wearing, only older and more ragged. Along with this, he dug out some old lined gloves. He did not say a word until Hampton was putting on his hat over by the desk, under Hank's impatient eye. When he started to give Hampton a warning his brother cut in with an impatient gesture and opened the jailhouse door. 'Come along, damn it all. We can argue on the way.'

They left the warm jailhouse with its cheery lamplight. Hampton's eyes had been accustomed to the light too long. He climbed aboard the cutter by feel rather than by sight, and as Hank urged the horses out into the rutted centre of the road, Hampton finished buttoning the coat and pulling on the gloves. It was freezing cold right there in town, with buildings on both sides to shelter the roadway, and that meant it would be much colder when they got out over the high meadow.

There were warm-lighted windows throughout Mandan. The buildings seemed to be crouching in the congealing cold, dark and low and square. Among the storefronts only two showed light, one was the gunsmith's little shop where a man was working inside at a bench, the other was the saloon, where storm-doors had replaced the batwing doors, and two soiled windows showed men hunched at the bar inside. Hampton looked in, then said, 'What excuse did that bunch of bastards have, Marshal?'

Ed did not reply. He was hunched inside his coat peering worriedly ahead where his brother was holding the strong, young team-horses to the ruts they had previously made. When he spoke he said, more to himself than to his companions, that at least this time the horses wouldn't have to break trail, which meant they'd still be strong when they got out as far as Hank and Ed had previously been. Hank and Hampton heard him say that and neither of them commented.

The night was utterly still. Every time a sled-runner crunched over ice it sounded like window-glass breaking. The air smelt of cold and woodsmoke, and the oncoming storm. Hampton lifted his face to the heavens, saw, then, how true Ed's prediction had been, and for the first time had a twinge of fear. A mile or two from town, in the kind of a blizzard that was building up overhead and which could break any moment, was the same as being a hundred miles out. If no one had volunteered to help before, they certainly would not offer to do so after the storm struck.

Hampton leaned forward over the back of the cutter's front seat and spoke to Hank. 'Where are the snowshoes?'

Hank answered without looking back. 'Behind the seat under the floorboard slats. I didn't have time to look at them. I hope to gawd the rawhide isn't rotten.'

Hampton hoped so too, as he twisted backwards and groped for the snowshoes. They were old and handmade, but they looked strong and durable. He shoved a pair at Ed and leaned to place the second pair up front beside Hank, then he moved around until he had room enough to put the third pair over his boots, and lash them into place. Ed watched. 'All right?' he asked. Hampton nodded, straightened up and felt the cold stiffen his face. He did not have a beard like Hank, not did he have a shawl to cover his head and face beneath his hat. His nose and ears were coldest, but Hampton had been through weather like this before. He knew the danger signals; as long as a man could feel his ears tingle he was safe. When they *stopped* tingling, he was in trouble.

The horses had power to spare, thus far, but they were still travelling through those ruts made earlier. Also, the horses could sense what was coming and that kept them alert. They would have turned-tail but for Hank's experienced hand on the lines. It was possible to see the steam of their breath, but visibility extended only a few yards beyond.

Ed raised his head like a turtle coming out of its shell. 'The only reason I took this damned job was for the extra money,' he said loudly. 'And right now I'd give it all back just to be next to the stove at the barn.'

Hank turned, grinning, his anxiety and impatience no longer prevalent, now that he was doing something, doing anything other than waiting and wondering. 'Spencer'll throw a fit if he happens to go down to the jailhouse tonight; then you won't have to quit, Ed, the Town Council will fire you.'

Ed grumbled. 'Wish I'd been fired this afternoon.' He bent to tie on the snowshoes and in the black hush Hampton heard him swear.

They covered that first mile in good time. Day-long warmth had lowered the height of the snow, in the open, flat places at any rate, but the new freeze had coated it with a glazed overlay of fine ice. What little light there was, came upwards as reflection off all that whiteness. In broad daylight it would have been blinding; this night, though, it helped visibilty at the same time it reminded the three men in the cutter that it was as deadly as any other natural excess could be.

Hank, who knew the countryside even when most landmarks were buried under snow, felt the lines slacken when they reached the end of the broken trail, and hauled his team down to a halt. The horses were willing to rest a moment and blow steam.

When Hank hooked his lines and reached for the snowshoes Hampton tapped his shoulder and shook his head. 'You stay with the rig,' he ordered. 'Ed and I'll mush ahead breaking trail. Give us enough of a lead as you can. If those damned horses get to lunging I don't want one of them climbing up my back. I'll whistle if I can't see you. That'll be your signal to follow us.'

Ed climbed out on the cutter's far side, Hampton got out on the near side. Both men tested their snowshoes without breaking through, which was encouraging, then they mushed up ahead by the horses and peered into the frigid darkness. Ed was not very hopeful. 'It'll be just plain luck if we find him out there.'

Hampton was thinking something different. If that man had been injured, had been unable to move and had been lying out there all day, he probably would have been able to survive because of the chinook-warmth. But for several hours now the temperature had been plummeting; an injured person, particularly if he could not move, by now would have suffered frostbite, at the very least. At worst, he could be dying while Hampton and Ed Teel snowshoed their way up the road following the hollow places where a horse had gone in the opposite direction hours earlier, the only tracks of any kind that the men encountered.

Hampton felt good. He could reach out to his full stride, even with the hampering snowshoes. He could swing his arms and fill his lungs. This was what freedom meant too a man like Hampton, even though it also meant death in a blizzard unless someone Up There was keeping an eye on him.

CHAPTER 8

Blizzard!

Ed Teel halted and breathed hard for a moment. He and Hampton were out of sight of Hank and the cutter, but it was so silent in the stygian darkness that all any of them had to do was speak in a normal tone and the other two could hear him. Hank, after losing sight of his brother and Hampton, could tell exactly where they were by the crunch of ice under snowshoes. When he thought they had broken enough trail he suggested that he drive that far ahead. Ed agreed, the horses lunged, the cutter's steel runners hissed, and out where Hampton stood watching, a big, fat snowflake fell and lingered on the back of his left hand. He ignored Hank and stared at that snowflake. Soon now, he told himself. Soon now they would have to either find their man and turn back, or turn back without their man. He called over to Ed. 'Fire a shot in the air.'

Ed obeyed, the noise hit low heaven and ricochetted, its waves of undulating echo bouncing back and forth until they faded far out in the darkness. The three men stood listening, even Hank, who was on his feet in the cutter. There was no answering gunshot.

Hampton did not share his thoughts with the others, he simply started mushing ahead again. Movement was better because the cold could not steal in when a man's body was active. After a quarter mile Ed Teel looked over and said, 'It's starting to snow.'

Hampton kept on swinging one foot, then the other foot. He was experienced with snow-shoes, but he still occasionally barked an ankle, and swore from the pain. He ignored Ed in order to conserve breath. Something drove him with a singular forcefulness. He got ahead of Ed and did not even look around until Ed called a breathless protest.

They covered another quarter mile and Hank drove over the blazed trail. They did that three times and had covered more than a mile. Hank traded places with Ed, who was tiring fast, and Hampton set the same pace for Hank. When he got a protest he said, 'Damn it, you see those flakes coming down? Well; I'm measuring the time it'll take for us to get back to Mandan from three miles out. If the flakes don't come faster, we can still make it, and if we poke along like a pair of old squaws we

87

aren't going to make it three miles out.'

Hank said, 'Yeah? And suppose our man's five miles out?'

Hampton grinned coldly. 'If you know that to be a fact, then we'd better speed it up, hadn't we?' But Hampton did not increase the pace and Hank ended his complaining. Actually, because of his beard, Hank was better off then the other two. Also, he was fresher, but Hampton tested him to the limit.

They were calling Ed to drive up the last quarter mile when Hampton heard a thin call, or thought he'd heard one. He faced into the lazy snowfall and waited until the cutter had halted, then he sang out.

'Call again! Keep calling!'

Hank and Ed looked at one another then at Hampton. Lastly, when the muffled wail came again, they looked ahead out into the northward darkness. Hank was re-energized and went swinging ahead, abreast of Hampton. Behind them, Ed kept the team ploughing along in the wake of the two men on snowshoes, neglectful of Hampton's earlier admonition about having the horses too close.

All three men could hear the cries now, even though they seemed to be weak. The snowfall was still light and sporadic, incapable of blanketing sound as yet.

In his mind's eye Hampton guessed they were past the westerly aspen grove where he had hid his saddlebags up a tree, and had to be somewhere near that pillar-rock he had seen and had forgotten all about until now. He said, 'Hank; where's the damned big rock?'

The answer came swiftly, along with a pointing arm. 'On your right and ahead maybe fifteen yards. If he made it behind that thing he got some shelter.'

Hampton held up a hand and stopped moving. 'Ed, turn the cutter around. Hank, help him so the horses don't flounder in the drifts off the roadbed. I'll go on up and see where that feller is.' Hampton did not wait to see whether he would be obeyed or not, he increased his gait, snowshoes notwithstanding, and behind him Hank and Ed stood watching until Hampton was lost up ahead, then, without a word, they started to manoeuvre the tight turnabout that would be necessary to head the cutter southward.

Hampton did not see the boulder until he was almost abreast of it because, now, the palm-sized snowflakes were increasing in frequency. The thin cry came from over there, on the east side of the pillar-stone. Hampton left the roadbed, and at once sank past his ankles even with the broad bearing-surfaces of his snowshoes. He found the man, and saw immediately why he had been able to survive this long. Before pulling the bridle and sending his horse towards town, the stranger had removed the bedroll from his saddle and was sitting there now, all hunched up under two wool blankets and a waterproof bedroll tarp.

Hampton leaned and looked into the drawn, white face. The man was a little grey with a weathered, lean face. He had a droopy long-horn moustache and light brown eyes beneath the snow-soaked brim of his hat. He smiled at Hampton and said, 'Mister, I never been so all-fired happy to see another human being in all my damned mis-spent life.'

Hampton pulled back the tarp. 'Can you stand up?'

The older man shook his head. 'Not very well. I got a busted leg. Broke it when I fell in the rocks over there while I was trying to see where the edge of the damned road was. Walking ahead of my horse; he was bushed from bucking the damned drifts.'

Hampton looked back, saw neither Hank nor Ed, then pulled the blankets off the stranger and spread his legs wide as he reached lower for the man's arm. 'Grit your teeth and heave up when I pull,' he said. 'Ready?'

The stranger came up in a one-legged stance

and groaned. Hampton got the stranger's right arm around his shoulders and gripped the stranger round the middle. The man's sixgun gouged and interfered so Hampton pulled it out and shoved it into his own waistband, then he said, 'Lean on me, mister, and hop. If you want to cuss, go right ahead. The cutter's down the road a piece.'

It was slow, hard work. They only had about sixty feet to cover until they reached Hampton's trail in the road but it required nearly fifteen minutes for them to make it, and afterwards even Hampton was ready to halt and blow. The stranger's face was sweat-shiny. His jaws bulged and his lips were bloodless from being forced flat with pain. But when they reached the tracks he smiled.

'You reckon this is payment for my sins?' he asked.

Hampton smiled, liking the stranger's toughness. 'If it is, mister, you sure must have racked up quite a score of them.

Hank appeared out of the snowfall and without a word got on the stranger's left side. Hank was a powerful man. Hampton could feel the load lighten very noticeably as he also gripped the injured man round the middle. They got back to the cutter and Ed helped them load the stranger. He flung an old moth-eaten buffalo robe from beneath the floor-slats over the man, then he turned and saw Hampton leaning on the cutter waiting to catch his breath. The saw-handle butt of the sixgun was clearly visible in Hampton's waistband.

Hank took the lines and got settled in the driver's seat. When his brother did not move to climb in, Hank turned with an impatient scowl. He too, saw the pistol-butt, and whatever he had been going to say, died on his lips.

Hampton finally straightened up. The stranger was slumped and loose under the old robe but Hank and Ed were not watching him, they were looking at Hampton. At first, Hampton was puzzled, then he remembered the gun. Both the Teels were armed and both had their coats buttoned over their holsters. There was no way for either of them to get at their holsters in time. They knew it and Hampton knew it.

He grinned, hauled out the stranger's Colt and offered it butt-first to Ed Teel. Ed turned his back and started to climb into the back seat with the injured man. 'I don't need it,' he said, and Hank raised his lines to flick them. Hampton climbed in beside Hank and the cutter started back through the increasing snowfall. All Hank said was: 'It's going to take more than skill if this snowfall gets any heavier, it's going to take a hell of a lot of luck.'

No one asked what he meant. No one had to. They were three miles or more from Mandan and the blizzard was beginning to cut visibility down to a horse's length up ahead.

Hank knew this road as well as anyone, but that would be helpful only as long as it was possible to tell by the burms on either side where the roadbed was beneath the snow. Hampton removed his snowshoes and massaged both his bruised ankles. 'You'll do it,' he told Hank, and maybe Hank also thought he might be able to do it, but he did not say so because he was too occupied with watching, not the tracks up ahead so much, because they were already beginning to fill with snow, but the two roadside little burms that told him where the edges were.

Ed removed his gloves and blew on his hands, rubbed them vigorously, then put the gloves back on and turned to look at the stranger. Hampton told him what the man had said and Ed bent to examine the man's legs. One of them had an unnatural cant to it. Ed set it square and the stranger groaned and seemed to rouse for a moment, but he only flickered a look around, then he slumped again and Ed shot Hampton a quick look.

'Colder'n a slab of frozen beef,' he said.

Hank finally stood up so he could see over the heads of the horses. The snowfall was getting heavier now, the flakes did not decrease in size, either, as they normally did in a blizzard. They were still big and soggy, only now they were only inches apart. It was almost impossible to see the ruts made by the cutter on the way out.

Hampton asked Hank how much farther they had to go, and got a tight answer. 'Might as well be fifty miles. I can't even see the edge of the damned road now, and the ruts are filling.'

Hampton leaned down to strap on his snowshoes again, Hank saw this and let the horses halt for a breather. As Hampton climbed out to mush ahead and lead the horses Hank shook his head. Whatever made him do that he kept to himself.

The horses were as lost and blinded as were the men in the cutter, but with Hampton mushing steadily up ahead the team had something to fix their sights on. They resumed their way with more confidence when Hank slapped their rumps and the cutter lurched ahead.

Now, Hampton did not need the exercise, but he was a strong individual and he was also experienced enough at hardships to pace himself. For as long as he could even dimly make out their former ruts he could stay to the centre of the road, but after what seemed hours of heart-straining slogging through fresh-fallen wet snow, the tracks showed as nothing more than a very vague set of imprints. He knew, but did not tell the others, that unless they found Mandan within the next twenty minutes, they were very likely going to be in serious trouble.

The horses leaned willingly into their collars; dumb-brute faith in the man out front kept them moving steadily in the right direction, but gradually, they became the only members of the rescue party who had much faith left. Even Hampton, when the ruts finally faded out up ahead, began to think in terms of being snow-smothered.

It was like being in the middle of an un-inhabited immensity of deathly silence that increased in its white depth as though to completely cover men, horses, and cutter. For each individual man, there was only the inner sound of his own heart for company.

Hampton paused, breathing hard, and squint-ed hard ahead. He saw a feeble orange glow! Hank also saw it from where he stood in the cutter and called ahead.

'Town! Hampton, so help me, you did it! We've made it!'

They had. In fact they were already abreast of the northernmost buildings without being able to see them because of the full force of a storm that now began to have wind-tremors behind it to make the big snow-flakes gyrate and whip inward to strike icily against their faces.'

Hampton started forward again, and in the cutter Ed also stood up to try and pick out landmarks. Only the injured stranger was past caring.

The wind increased to a low-moaning, snow-flakes stung, now, when they hit faces, and Hampton saw a carriage lamp that he remembered was outside the front opening of Ed Teel's liverybarn. He turned, stumbling blindly, finally, and when he felt wooden boards under his out-stretched hand, he stepped aside and let the cutter precede him into the icy interior of the big old barn.

CHAPTER 9

A Grey Morning

Ed Teel's hostler was nowhere around. Ed said he was probably up at the saloon where the other unattached men in town usually congregated, even on pleasant nights, for a few drinks and fan-tan or poker, or maybe a few hands of Pedro.

Hank and Ed got the injured man to the cot in Ed's harnessroom while Hampton built a fire in the little iron stove. The cot was where Ed's hostler slept, but for the time being no one thought much about that.

When they had the man's shell belt, hat and boots removed, the room began to get warm. Hank examined the stranger's feet and pronounced him free of frostbite, but it was a miracle.

Ed slit the man's trouser-leg and they all saw the break; the flesh was splotchy-purple but, probably because of the intense cold, there was scarcely any swelling.

Hampton went to the box of kindling wood

beside the hot little stove and sighted down a number of pieces of wood until he found a pair of acceptable splints, then wordlessly handed them to Hank, who stood looking down at the pieces of wood as though he had never seen anything like them before. Ed took them and dropped to one knee beside the cot.

'Tear me some strips for bindings,' Ed told his brother, nodding towards an old frayed tarpaulin hanging amidst the harness. Hank went to work and Hampton stood with his back to the stove feeling blessed heat baking through the soggy old blanket-coat, through tightly knotted muscles all the way to his bone-marrow. He closed his eyes and thought that if he'd had a choice, this is right where he would like to spend Eternity; in front of a crackling little iron stove in a room that smelled of sage and horses and leather.

When Ed finished he asked Hampton to look over his work. 'I've splinted a few canon bones from time to time, but never before on two-legged critters.'

Hampton thought the splint was good enough, but he had only helped set one other broken leg so, as he said, he was anything but an authority. Then he turned, lifted the sixgun from his waistband and dropped it indifferently into the stranger's holster where one of the

Teel's had hung the shell belt from a harness hook. He turned back, saw both brothers watching him, and said, 'I am going up to the jailhouse to bed.'

Ed was finished with the stranger. Hank said he would sit awhile with the man, and if it seemed the stranger would be all right, he would be along after a bit. Then he smiled at Hampton. 'The quart of whisky is in the lower desk drawer. Just save me a drink.'

The moment Ed and Hampton stepped back out into the runway, icy wind made them gasp and duck their heads. In the roadway yonder, snow was flying in all directions with visibility limited to three or four feet. Ed said something but Hampton could not make it out as they leaned to buck their way forward, hurling their weight behind each onward step.

The drifts were higher now, and they reached mid-way up the fronts of buildings, but directly beneath the plank-walk overhang, for some bizarre reason, the wind had swept the scuffed planking almost bare, which was a god-send, because fighting the wind was bad enough without also having to fight fresh snowdrifts.

It took longer to get from the liverybarn to the jailhouse on this night than it ordinarily took to walk from one end of Mandan to the

99

other end. When Hampton finally reached the doorway he was breathing almost as hard as he'd breathed after guiding the cutter's team the last mile to town.

Inside, the cold had seeped through despite the fact that the stove was still giving off heat. Ed had to lean on the door to hold it closed until he could latch it. Afterwards, he stepped across to the stove and stoked it from the wood-box, and as he struggled out of his soggy coat Hampton was already draping his soaked and brittle old outer garment across the back of a chair. Then he went rummaging for the whisky.

Without a word being said both men lifted their waterglasses and let liquid warmth flow downward and outward until the cold-induced stiffness began to abate. As Hampton lowered the glass he eyed the straw-filled mattress on his cell bunk and got an ironic twinkle in his dark eyes.

'That's the best-looking bed I ever saw,' he told Ed, and crossed to the cell, closed the door after himself, then picked up the key off the bunk and flipped it out through the bars. 'Lock me in, Marshal, and no matter what I volunteer to do next time, don't you dare unlock that door.'

Ed laughed, picked up the key and locked

the cell door. He stood outside with his half-empty glass in one hand, the big key in his other. 'Mister—whatever-your-name is—for my brother and me. Much obliged. I reckon the stanger'll thank you when he can.'

Hampton looked up. 'Go to hell. You and your brother and the stranger.' He smiled and lay back full length on the bunk. 'You know something, Ed? That was damned awful close.'

Teel did not respond. He finished his whisky and went over to sit at his desk. 'I ache in places I never ached in before in my whole cussed life.'

Hampton raised both thick arms and clasped his hands beneath his head. 'Did you know that gun was empty?'

Ed looked long, in through the bars. 'I didn't know that.'

'You should have. When you fired he didn't fire back, did he?'

Ed swore. 'I'll be damned. I never thought of that.'

Hampton looked over, smiling. 'Neither did I, until I put the gun in his holster. Then I remembered and looked. Sure enough, he'd fired all six chambers empty. Probably during the day.' Hampton kept smiling. 'Wouldn't have done me any good, even if I'd had a horse and there hadn't been any snow.'

Teel thought a moment before speaking again. 'Tell me the truth. Hampton, would you have made the attempt, if things had been different?'

The black-eyed prisoner's smile faded out and he lay back again. 'That's a hell of a question, Marshal...I don't know. I passed you my word I'd come back with you. Maybe I would have kept it. You know, a poor man's really only got his self-respect.' His smile jumped up again. 'On the other hand, what the hell good is self-respect to a man dangling ten feet off the ground with a busted neck?'

Hank arrived during the lull that followed this exchange. Ed's hostler had returned. Hank laughed in recollection. 'You should have seen the look on his face when he came through that harnessroom door. He said everyone was sure you and me had frozen to death up the stageroad somewhere. He was so surprised he forgot to ask where he was supposed to sleep, what with the stranger passed out on his cot.'

Hampton listened, then asked if Hank had looked through the stranger's pockets for identification. Hank hadn't, he said, but when the stranger had opened his eyes once, had tried to sit up, Hank had got a couple of swallows of liquor down the man.

Outside, the wind had the snow flying in all

directions as it rattled doors and windows and tore at rafter-ends. Even the stone-walled jailhouse was made to quiver from an occasional blast. Inside, Hampton recalled the first storm and decided that regardless of what the natives had said, the other storm had only been a prelude to this one. *This* was the real blizzard.

He began feeling drowsy, the heat had built up unnoticed until the jailhouse was as pleasantly stuffy as it could be, and it also helped that Hampton had been bitterly cold and physically worn down when he had returned with Ed Teel. He slept. Ed and Hank Teel made the jailhouse ready for a long night, were not particularly quiet as they went about it, and eventually they left, locking the jailhouse door from outside.

The storm did not abate. Mandan huddled throughout that bitter night, and by morning, when the wind died, some unique inconsistencies were visible by the watery-white firstlight. One of them was that the wind had scrubbed the roadway almost clean of any trace of snow; it had then piled drifts in some places as high as six feet, and it had sculpted them into some unbelievably weird shapes. Gradually, though, after the wind fled and the snowfall continued, the roadway acquired a fresh white covering. In fact by morning, what had been a nightmare of wind and unusual wildness, was a very ordinary snowstorm with large, fleecy flakes coming down with delicate drift and silent beauty, and the storm-scent was there, as usual, along with the deathly stillness.

Again, Hampton slept past sunrise, probably because there was no sun, was, in fact, scarcely any change in the tone of daylight from firstlight until high noon. The world was the shade of old blue steel one occasionally saw in a saddlegun. It carried no lustre, had no reflections, and where a miasmic mist did not prevail, there was a low-bellied sky with dark streaks like swollen arteries running all across it.

When Ed Teel finished at the liverybarn and hurried to get Hampton's breakfast from the café and take it to the jailhouse, his prisoner was only just stirring. By the time Ed had stoked the stove, turned off the lamp, shed his hat and coat and gloves, Hampton had finished making himself presentable, had stood a moment by the rearwall window looking at the weird pillars and mushrooms the wind had carved, and had discovered that his shoulders and legs and back ached.

He asked how the stranger was and all Ed Teel could tell him was that before retiring last night Ed had looked in on him, and the stranger had been sleeping like a log, but that this morning he hadn't had time to do more than glance in because he and his hostler had had enough to keep them busy until he'd arrived at the jailhouse, shovelling a pathway for Teel's horses to get out into the corrals from their barn-stalls.

Hampton picked up the breakfast pan from under the door as he said, 'That was quite a work-out last night.'

Ed agreed. Then he said, 'You should see the town. You should also see the road northward beyond town—in fact you ought to see the whole damned countryside. It's like the moon, or something, with us squatting out here in the middle of it.'

Ed went after a bucket of snow which he set beside the stove to melt. While he waited for this to happen he rinsed out the coffee pot and flung in a cupful of coarse grounds from a cloth coffee sack. By then the snow had melted, so he finished making a fresh pot, and set it atop the stove.

Hampton finished eating and smoked in comfort. He'd had an uncharitable thought upon awakening this morning. It concerned something Hank had said the night before. 'I reckon most towns are alike,' he said to Ed Teel, 'but last night when those men were betting you and your brother were freezing to death, lost in the blizzard, like your hostler said they were doing up at the saloon, I wonder if any of them even thought about getting up a rescue party.'

Ed went over to sit behind the desk before saying anything. 'You answered that when you said most towns are alike. I don't know who-all was up there last night, but probably the usual bunch of loafers. Most of them wouldn't have joined a rescue party; without leadership probably none of them would have. But whether they did or didn't wouldn't have made much difference. Hampton, not after we turned back for town, because our tracks were covered over by them. All they knew, I reckon, was that we'd decided to make another attempt to find some lost stranger.' Ed Teel smiled. 'Hank and me. We were lucky as hell no one wanted to look at you bad enough during the storm and while we were out there with the cutter, to buck the wind and snow and come look in, down here. Folks think it was just Hank and me that went out after the stranger the second time like we did the first time.'

Right then, this seemed to have no special significance to Hampton. He even smiled back and said, 'Saved your job. What your Town

Council don't know they won't fire you about.'

The coffee boiled and filled the jailhouse with a pleasant smell. Ed went to fill two cups. While he was about this, his brother arrived bundled against the cold, winked and nodded at Hampton, then said, 'I thought you fellers was all wrapped up in one of those checker sessions and had plumb forgot.'

Ed was handing a cup through the bars to Hampton when he said, 'Forgot what?'

'Hampton's trial. I just met some of the fellers from around town stamping through the drifts in the direction of Abe Spencer's backroom.'

Ed had completely forgot. Whether Hampton had also forgot was difficult to tell from his expression as he stood inside his cell holding the cup of coffee looking out at Hank Teel with an expression of dark impassivity.

CHAPTER 10

The Face of Legal Murder

A lot of things had been changing even before the storm, but during it, and even after it while Mandan was still storm-bound and cut off, people's lives had assumed a distinctiveness, a largeness and total significance, they could not have had before because while Mandan was part of the outside world, connected to it by stages and telegraph facilities, external events always tended to diminish individual importance. Now, although no one seemed aware yet, the outside world was completely incapable of intervening, so the people were dependent upon their own resources, they had neither nation nor state. No one could help them but they, themselves. They were tribesmen exactly as the oldtime Indians who had once roamed their countryside had been.

When Hank had reminded his brother and his brother's prisoner that Able Spencer still meant to hold court despite the storm and despite everything else, the most significant change at the jailhouse was the attitude of the men inside it towards one another. If familiarity bred contempt, it also bred respect.

Ed went to the front window and kept looking out as he said, 'You ready, Hampton?'

The prisoner tasted his coffee before replying. It was black and acidy. 'I reckon so,' he said, and winked solemnly at Hank. 'Spencer may be doing me a favour; I won't have to finish this damned coffee.'

Ed went woodenly for the key and opened the cell. He waited for the prisoner to dump the hat on the back of his head and stand in the centre of the little outer office before he shrugged into his own coat and hat. He was having unpleasant thoughts, which showed across his face, but he said nothing even after the three of them left the jailhouse and started towards the upper end of town. Hank bringing up the rear, hands plunged deep into coat pockets, head sucked low inside a turned-up collar. It was cold and snow still fell. The roadway was no longer bare, but had about three or four inches covering its wide surface, and kids bundled to the ears were out there shouting in rapture as they sought with mittened hands to improve on some of the weird snow-silhouettes the wind had carved.

Hampton, listening to the piping voices, said,

'It's little like Christmas, isn't it?' to Ed Teel, who was staring gravely up at the milling crowd out front of the stage-line office. Ed answered absently.

'Yeah. Couple of months and it'll be here.'

Their breath steamed and their faces reddened, all but Hank's face, but whiskers could not protect his nose and when it tingled from cold he removed a glove and rubbed it.

Ed did not take his prisoner through the staring, silent throng out front, he guided him around back to the only outside door that gave access to the room Abel Spencer called his courtroom.

The stove was a big, army cannon heater, large enough to keep a barracks warm. It had evidently been crackling and popping for some time because the moment Hampton stepped past the door he felt a wave of warmth engulf him.

There were benches for spectators and near the door leading through so the stage-line office out front, there was a high-backed chair with black leather upholstery, and a table with three lawbooks standing upright, spines to the spectators, held in place by two large pieces of veined quartz. On the wall behind the black-leather chair was a lithograph of George Washington, and next to him was one of Abraham

Lincoln. In a corner was a droopy flag standing in an urn filled with sand.

Hank went to a wall-bench and unbuttoned his coat, pulled off his hat and gloves, and watched his brother and the prisoner take two chairs to the right of the judge's seat. As though Ed's arrival with the prisoner were the cue, people, almost exclusively men, shuffled through from out front. A few, but not many, entered and took seats along the benches by the rear door, the one though which Hampton had arrived. That door opened inward off the corral yard where the stage-line's horses and coaches and repair shops formed a large, fort-like square behind Spencer's big slab-sided building.

Hampton turned and watched the benches fill up. He met looks of frank interest, suspicion, antagonism, and mild curiosity. Just about every reason people had for sitting in on a trial, was in those cold-reddened rough faces, including an expression of pleasant indifference as though those men were only there because they knew the room would be comfortably warm, and they had no place else to loaf.

When Abel Spencer came through from out front he was wearing a black coat, a black string tie, and a pair of steel-rimmed glasses that made his marble-like slately little eyes look a lot more

111

benign than Hampton remembered them. Spencer looked at the prisoner from an expressionless face, and Hampton felt the rancour as though it were something solid, something insurmountable. He leaned and spoke quietly to Ed.

'Hell, he can't be the only lawyer, can he? Don't I get representation?'

Ed answered quickly in an even lower tone. 'This is just the preliminary hearing, it's not really a trial. Folks call it a trial because they don't know any better. You see, before you can really be brought to trial, it has to be established by this kind of a hearing—by a justice court preliminary determination, it's called in my law book—that a crime has in fact been committed, and that you are very likely the feller that committed it. Once that's established, then you are bound over, which means you go back to the jailhouse, until the regular trial.'

Hampton thought about that. It sounded reasonable; needlessly complicated, but reasonable. He knew nothing about the law from first-hand experience, but he'd read enough in newspapers to have some idea that the judicial processes were pretty damned involved. Right now, he was relieved to know that the look in Abell Spencer's eyes would be unable to condemn him; he knew men well enough to know that was what Spencer's look meant.

Court was called to order when Spencer hit a stone with a wooden gavel, then read off the allegations and pointed at Hampton as the accused. 'The bay horse is down at Teel's livery-barn, impounded as evidence, and we have a wire from a Wyoming sheriff describing the horse, so we can be certain that this is the right animal. We also know, because a lot of folks saw this feller ride him into town, that this prisoner brought the bay horse to Mandan township.' Spencer paused to look directly at Hampton. 'We got enough facts to make out a case of the folks of Mandan township against this feller who says his name is Hampton, for horsestealing.'

The room was deathly still except for the crackling fire in the potbellied cannon heater. Without taking his eyes off Abel Spencer, Hampton knew every spectator was staring at him. Ed was sitting relaxed at his side, but Hampton did not relax; he knew very little about the law, even after Ed had explained this part of it to him, but deep down he began to have a bad feeling, a frightening premonition. The uncompromising rancour in Spencer's stare caused him to begin to have doubts. Abel Spencer was not acting like a judge who was trying to sift through allegations to reach facts,

113

he acted more like a man who was already convinced. He had acted that way before, when he had first visited the jailhouse after Hampton was locked up.

Spencer removed his glasses and looked out over the little crowded room. He was king here, there was no doubt about that, and none of the men in his courtroom excepting the Teel brothers, had so much as spoken to the prisoner. To them, it was Abel Spencer's word against the word of a horsethief.

Then Spencer spoke on, but now his voice was different; it was hard and flat and menacing. 'This man committed his crime up in Wyoming, but we can't send him up there because we're snowed in, and they can't get down here, so that places the responsibility for trying him on this here court.'

Hampton felt Ed Teel stiffen in the chair next to him. 'And we got enough evidence,' Spencer announced, avoidingn Ed Teel's stare, 'to conclude here and now that the preliminary hearing is concluded.' Spencer hit the stone again with his gavel, waited several seconds, then struck the stone again as he said, 'And that the criminal trial is now in progress.' Finally, in the hush, Spencer brought his icy stare around to Ed Teel. 'Marshal, take the Bible and swear in the prisoner.'

Teel did not move. Hampton looked at him. Ed and the judge were looking steadily at one another. Spencer's little pursed lips drew out into a lipless wound and his slatey eyes bored in with an almost fanatical coldness.

'Marshal, I said swear in the prisoner!'

Teel leaned forward and stood up. 'What the hell are you trying to do?' he exclaimed. 'Abel, this here is a preliminary hearing. You can't make a trial out of it until—'

'Are you deaf!' Spencer spat. 'I said we just concluded the preliminary hearing. Now we're going to try this damned horsethief. Now Ed, you swear him in!'

Teel looked like he was out of breath. He had been caught unprepared, had been caught off-guard, and for the drawn out moment while he groped for words, Hampton knew at last that his earlier premonition had been accurate. It did not surprise him. He had sized up Abel Spencer at that first meeting at the jailhouse. But now, he knew the answer to that question Ed had asked him the night before, about whether he would have used the gun to gain his freedom. Only now it was too late.

Spencer spoke into the complete silence, with every eye on him. 'Ed, you either swear in the prisoner or take off your badge. I know you been favouring this damned outlaw. You've

115

shown ignorance of the law before and this here court has overlooked it, but not this time.'

Ed responded, finally, in an angry outburst. 'Hell, Abel, the prisoner's entitled to a defence. You've got to prove he didn't trade for the horse like he says he did. That's the purpose of a preliminary hearing; this court's got to show beyond a reasonable doubt that Hampton could be guilty.' Spencer shot back his answer, and the spectators were entranced at this fight between the authorities of their township. 'This here court has already proved Hampton stole the horse.' Spencer held aloft the telegram from Wyoming. 'This proves that the horse was stolen.' Spencer pointed at Hampton with a rigid finger. 'We've got witnesses that saw that feller ride into town on the stolen horse.' Spencer lowered his arm and smiled at Ed Teel. 'And there are three cattlemen right out there among the spectators who have been hunting strays for the past ten days up along the northerly foothills who will swear they never saw a single rider they didn't know, and that's good enough proof that Hampton didn't meet anyone and trade horses with them. Now, for the last time, Ed, by gawd you swear that man in!'

Ed said, 'But Hampton never claimed he traded for the horse around here, Abel. And even if he had, according to my law book he's entitled to legal counsel. You can't just switch your gavel from your right hand to your left hand and declare a trial in progress.'

'I've already done it,' snarled Abel Spencer, and looked out over the motionless spectators until he found the man he sought. 'Henry Meachem, you are hereby appointed by this here court temporary town marshal, replacing Ed Teel. Come forward and be sworn in. Then take the Bible and—'

Ed whirled as a large, shaggy-headed man in a blanket-coat stood up half smiling, half sneering. 'You keep out of this, Henry. Abel can't try Hampton even if he has good proof, which he doesn't have. That damned horse wasn't stolen around here, he was stolen up in Wyoming.'

Meacham was a hard-faced, scarred, bullying-type. His muddy eyes showed a sneer as he swept back his coat and hooked it under an exposed shellbelt. 'Abel's the law,' he said in a growling voice that was deep and truculent. 'You just been replaced, Ed, so don't go and make it no worse for yourself.' Meacham edged past into the aisle and sauntered towards the front of the courtroom, thick, sloping shoulders rolling in a swagger. He smiled down into Abel Spencer's tilted face. 'Give me that Bible, Abel.'

Ed stood like a stone statue. Behind him Hampton heard the first murmur among the spectators, but he could not decided whether it favoured Ed or Judge Spencer. He did not know these people, but thinking back to their lack of concern the previous night when he and the Teels had risked their lives, he decided the murmur was in favour of the big cowboy named Meachem and the fanatical man sitting in judgement on him.

Over against the far wall Hank was white and utterly still. He was crowded in close between two other men, older than Hank, who looked pleased with the way things were going. To most rangemen the worst kind of an outlaw was a horsethief.

Hampton tried to believe what was happening involved him, and despite his ignorance of legal procedure, he knew he had been correct when he'd told Ed to shoot him. Abel Spencer was going to see him hanged before evening!

CHAPTER 11

Backfire!

The room was hot now, as much from the crowd of bodies as from the heat of the stove. Ed had been forced to a subordinate role even though he still stood beside Hampton, who had made his appraisal of Henry Meachem, the big, mean-faced cowboy. When Meacham turned with a bold stare, Hampton unwound up out of his chair. This checked the new town marshal. He looked at Hampton evidently coming to some kind of decision about the dark-eyed prisoner; Meacham hesitated. In the electric silence Spencer said, 'Swear him in, Henry! Ed, you and Hampton be damned careful. I figured something like this might crop up. I got four men in the back of the room with shotguns. All right, Henry...'

Meacham and Hampton were the same height but Meachem was thicker, coarser made. Every town Hampton had ever been in, as well every ranch and riding crew, had a Meacham; tough men, overbearing, never cowards but never popular, bullies, hard-drinkers, men who spoiled for trouble and were loud.

Meacham's face, up close, was brutish and scarred. His muddy eyes were set close and his forehead was low and narrow. Meacham was the kind of man who followed an order without questioning, without actually caring, whether it was right or wrong.

He held out the Bible. 'Put your right hand on this here book,' he growled at Hampton, and when the prisoner made no move to obey, the muddy eyes narrowed because this was something Henry Meacham understood. He knew nothing of the law, but he knew all about personal defiance. 'Horsethief, you put your damned hand on this here book or I'll put it on there for you!'

Hampton's black eyes were stone steady as he stood silent and motionless.

Abel Spencer, leaning to see around Meachem, finally had to get to his feet. He was moving to a better point of vantage when the rear door opened and a man entered wearing a bright blue blanket-coat and a soggy black hat. He was on crutches and behind him was Ed Teel's worried-looking hostler. Hampton did not turn and neither did Henry Meachem, but Ed and Hank, and almost everyone else,

120

turned. Even Judge Spencer looked around, but his expression showed quick indignation. The newcomer had arrived at a very bad time. Spencer waited until the man hitched himself inside, then he snarled at the hostler, saying, 'Close that damned door and lock it from inside, we'll have no more confounded interruptions to this here trial.'

The shaking hostler obeyed but the man on the crutches made no move to sit. He jockeyed himself over to the nearest rear wall and leaned back, his one supporting leg bearing all the weight. Abel glared. 'Find a seat, stranger, and set.'

The injured man did not move, once he was settled against the wall, and he did not look as though he liked Able Spencer's tone of voice. 'This feller from the liverybarn told me you were trying a horsethief up here this morning,' he said in a quiet voice, and every head turned as the newcomer usurped everyone's attention. Ed and Hank and Hampton recognized the stranger at once but no one else did; he was the injured man they had brought in last night with the broken leg, and although he still looked pale and drawn out, he also looked as though when he spoke he was accustomed to being listened to.

Abel Spencer got exasperated. 'That's right,

mister, we're trying a horsethief. Now take a seat and shut up.'

The stranger's droopy moustache stiffened as the man raised a hand to run under it. He shook his head at Spencer. 'Where's the horse-thief?'

Spencer reddened. 'There! That quarter-breed-looking lanky feller. Now damn it all, you sit down and shut up!'

The stranger said, 'I don't think so, Judge.'

Everyone had lost interest in Hampton and Meachem. An old cowman called out. 'You don't think what, mister?'

'I don't think you have a horsethief in this room,' the stranger replied. 'I was on my way down here and got caught in that damned bliz-zard.'

Ed spoke up with a ring of fresh hope. 'You're from Wyoming?'

The stranger nodded. 'Yup.'

'You're the sheriff who sent us the wire about that stolen horse?'

The stranger slowly shook his head. 'No. I'm the feller who *owned* that horse. My name is Hugh R. Deming. That's my brand on the horse's neck under the mane. I was already down near here arranging to buy some mares when I got a wire from the sheriff up home saying you folks had my horse down here, and the thief.'

Abel Spencer rapped for order because the room suddenly buzzed with excited talk. When it was quiet again Spencer said, 'You got proof of your identity, mister?'

The stranger fished in a pocket and brought forth a wallet and some letters. 'Plenty of proof, Judge.' He turned and looked impassively at Hampton, then at Ed Teel. 'You boys are pretty close to making a damned bad mistake. That man didn't steal my thoroughbred gelding ...I *gave* it to him. Right here in my hand is the bill of sale. He pulled out before I could give it to him.'

For a moment it seemed that everyone in the room held their breath, even Abel Spencer. Then Henry Meachem lowered the Bible and turned to await whatever Abel Spencer had to say.

For a while the judge leaned on his desk staring towards the back of the room. 'How'd you get here,' he demanded, 'and how'd you hurt your leg?'

'Busted the leg on some ice yesterday, Judge, and last night that feller and two more found me and brought me back to town in a cutter.'

Spencer straightened up. 'You mean—*Hampton* and two other fellers brought you back?'

'Yes,' said the stranger. 'One of them was

the man wearing the badge standing next to Hampton. The third one, I don't see.'

Over against the wall Hank stood up. This movement caught the stranger's eye and he pointed. 'That's the third man.'

Abel Spencer sat down very gently. He looked at Ed almost benevolently. 'You turned the prisoner out last night, did you?'

Before Ed could answer Hank spoke out for the first time. 'Abel, you wouldn't come along and I couldn't get anyone else. We needed a third hand.'

'So you released an outlaw,' said Spencer. 'You deliberately turned that man loose when you know damned well he was supposed to be locked up. Ed, I told you he wasn't eligible for bail, but your turned him loose anyway.'

The big stranger broke in. 'Wait a minute, Judge. I told you—that man is no horsethief, so if you had him locked up on such a charge, you had him incarcerated wrongfully.'

Hampton studied the stranger. Last night he had looked like a soaked, freezing, half-dead cowboy. Today, in dry, fresh clothing using words that sounded like he might know a little law, he looked altogether different. As for that story about having sold the bay horse to Hampton, it was a bald lie from start to finish, but it was not hard to guess why the stranger had told it. He'd had it from Ed Teel's hostler down at the liverybarn, who had saved his life last night, and now he was here to repay the debt.

Spencer sat back in his black leather chair and pinched his small lips together as he steadily eyed the newcomer. Then, when he rocked forward to speak, he was the centre of attention again, because what he said drove a fresh wedge of doubt among the spectators.

'I'll tell you what I think, stranger; I figure you're Hampton's partner, and that you cooked this up to save him from hanging, and unless you can damned well convince this here court otherwise, you're awful close to going to the hang-tree with your partner.'

Ed Teel straightened around towards Spencer's desk. Even Hampton, who was more sanguinary, was surprised. 'I never had a partner,' he said to Abel Spencer, and Henry Meachem snarled Hampton into silence.

'You shut up! Don't you open your mouth again unless you're spoken to!'

Spencer smiled. 'Henry, you take Ed and the prisoner...*and* that feller with the busted leg too...and you lock 'em up in the jailhouse. You put on the town marshal's badge and you don't open that cell door until tomorrow morning when we'll re-convene this here court—and

125

then, by gawd, we'll try *two* outlaws instead of just one.'

Ed stood staring at Abel Spencer even after most of the spectators, mumbling back and forth, had begun to file out of the hot little room. He did not move until Hampton elbowed him and turned to follow the others out. Behind Hampton was Henry Meachem with his palmed sixgun, and back by the rear door were two men with shotguns on each side of Hugh Deming.

The only one who had spoken out and who had not been involved in the aftermath of the preliminary hearing, and the attempted court trial, was Hank Teel. He filed out with the other spectators, quite unheeded.

Abel Spencer arose with his steel-rimmed glasses in his hand. He gave Ed a malevolently triumphant glare, then marched back towards the front office of his building.

Henry Meachem growled and Ed finally moved. To Hampton, it seemed that Ed was still suffering from shock. As far as Hampton was concerned, though, despite the irregularities, and whatever else Deming's intentions had been one thing stood out. They would not hang him tonight. When a man saw himself that close to death even a delay of a day and a night were an equivalent to a fresh toehold, a fresh chance. He went along with Ed and Deming, none of them saying a word, while four armed townsmen following the new town marshal, herded them through a steamy-breathed, closed faced throng of onlookers in the direction of the jailhouse.

It was more than simply ironic that Ed, who had left this same building only an hour or a little earlier as town marshal, was now returning to it not as just a discredited lawman, but also as a prisoner.

But to Hampton the most unbelievable fact was that the man he and the Teels had saved from certain death last night, had not only turned out to be the owner of the bay gelding, but had also been accused of being an outlaw.

When they reached the jailhouse and Meachem growled at the armed townsmen to depart, those men seemed perfectly willing to have no more to do with this matter and went back the way they had come. Inside, Meachem asked where the cell-door key was, and after Ed told him, he disarmed Teel, searched the stranger, emptied his pockets, then herded those two into the cell along with Hampton, locked the door, and afterwards stood back looking triumphantly in at his prisoners.

'The badge,' he said to Ed. 'Take it off and toss it out here.'

Teel obeyed. He flung the badge over into a far corner of the outer office then turned his back. Meachem's face got red but he said nothing until he had retrieved the badge and was pinning it to his jacket. Then he laughed at Ed Teel.

'You were plain stupid, Ed. Judge Spencer figured everything just like you done it. He told me last night what he was going to do—bait you into bucking the court—and I'll be damned if he didn't badger you into doing it just like he figured.'

Hampton leaned on the rear wall and made a smoke. When he had it lighted he gazed almost dispassionately out through the bars. 'I'll tell you something, Meachem,' he said softly. 'That judge of yours is crazy. Plumb crazy, and if you've got a lick of sense you'll cut loose from him before he gets you shot.'

Meachem swaggered closer to the bars. 'Who's going to shoot me, horsethief? You? Like hell. These other two friends of yours?' Meachem laughed and shook his head at Hampton. 'By this time tomorrow, horsethief, the only one still able to stand up will be Ed Teel. And I wouldn't want to bet much money the judge won't find a legal reason for stretching his lousy neck too.'

Hampton said no more, but he stood back

128

there watching every move Henry Meachem made. Deming, on the other hand, who had said nothing since leaving the courtroom, sat on the cell's single wall-bunk and propped his splinted leg straight out. He seemed neither as coldly and murderously bitter as Hampton was, nor as dumbfounded and shocked as Ed Teel was.

In fact, Deming put aside his hat and leaned back to get comfortable, his entire body relaxed and loose. He seemed to be more sceptical than outraged, and that was unusual because he most certainly could not have anticipated the reaction his story would have caused in Abel Spencer's courtroom. But so far, no one around Mandan knew anything about Hugh Deming except that he had been saved from death the previous night, had a broken leg, and claimed to be the rancher from up north who owned that stolen bay horse with the HRD brand on his neck.

CHAPTER 12

A Glimmer of Hope

Not until Henry Meachem went up to the café to get three tin plates of food for his prisoners, for supper, did Hampton and Teel speak frankly to their cell-mate, Deming.

When they asked him to verify what he had said in Abel Spencer's court, Deming obliged. He had been over at a town called Craig looking at some breedy mares, when he had been informed by telegraph where his stolen bay horse was. He had ridden out of Craig the very next morning, and even though it had looked threatening and he had been warned in Craig a storm was brewing, he had felt confident of reaching Mandan before it broke.

'You know the rest of that story,' he said to Ed and Hampton. Then he looked steadily at Hampton. 'Okay, cowboy; I owed you as much as I tried to do this morning. You saved my bacon so I tried to save yours.' Deming smiled with hard irony. 'Looks like I not only didn't help you a damned bit, but it looks like I

130

landed myself in bad trouble too.' Deming shrugged that off and transferred his attention to Ed Teel. 'It looks to me like your town's got a problem, Marshal. It looks to me like your judge is unbalanced.'

Before Ed could say anything Hampton spoke. 'Mister Deming, Ed's *town* doesn't have a problem, *we* have a problem, the three of us have a problem. Spencer is going to hang me sure as shooting; maybe he was trying to scare you, but whatever his reason for having you locked up, Meachem seemd to figure the judge might hang you tomorrow right along with me. Whether Judge Spencer is crazy or not doesn't worry me nearly as much as still being in this jailhouse come morning.'

Deming and Ed let Hampton get it all said before either of them spoke, then Ed pointed to the rear wall window and the white paleness visible beyond. 'If you escaped, Hampton—if all *three* of us escaped—it's still the same outside as when you and I talked of this before: Where the hell could we go that Abe Spencer and a damned posse of idiots wouldn't dig us out?'

Hampton shot his answer right back. 'Maybe nowhere, Ed, but we're not going anywhere inside this jailhouse, either, are we? If we could bust out, slim as the chance of surviving might

131

be, it sure as hell would be a lot better than what we got in here.'

Deming held up a hand. 'Hampton is right. But that doesn't help much because no one's explained to me yet, just how we get out of here. How about catching our jailer when he returns with supper?'

Ed knew better. He had been shoving food under the cell door long enough to know that unless someone on the outside got up very close to the bars, the man inside could not reach him. 'No chance,' he said to Hugh Deming.

Deming was not upset. 'All right, if that won't work what will? There's got to be a way out, Teel, and you'd be the one who'd know what it is.'

Ed looked almost apologetic as he said, 'No way. There's no way under the sun to bust out of this cell. My brother and I designed it, and he built and installed it. We tried every way we knew, to figure a way to break out. There just is no way.'

Deming looked up at Hampton. 'So we hang,' he said, and watched Hampton make a cigarette. When Hampton lit up and turned towards the alley window to lean, looking out, Deming frowned at his splinted leg propped out front of him. For a few moments he was content to stay silent, and even afterwards, when the three of them resumed their discussion, Deming was changed; he was a lot less confident, a lot less assured and relaxed. Perhaps he had thought, earlier, that his situation was too bizarre to be really dangerous. If he did think that he'd had good cause. But now, locked in an escape-proof jail cell, bound over to be tried as a felon the following morning and very probably to be hanged afterwards, there was no way to keep his earlier aplomb.

He said, 'Teel, it's hard to believe that crazy judge could have the entire town on his side.'

It wasn't hard to believe, for Ed. In the first place, Abel had been sitting as the justice court judge for enough years to have the confidence of the local people. In the second place, as Ed told Deming, the people knew nothing about the law, except that if a man broke it he usually was arrested, tried, and punished. 'They are perfectly content to let Abel handle things his way, and if he tells them to stand in the back of his courtroom with scatter-guns, they do it.'

From the window Hampton said. 'And if they are told to haul hard on a lynchrope...?' He turned, facing Ed Teel.

Ed nodded. 'They'll do it.'

Hampton dropped his glance to the seated man. 'I been figuring, and it seems to me that

133

crazy devil has been out-foxing us right down the line. Mister Deming, where is that bill-of-sale you drew up on that bay horse I stole from you?'

As Deming answered, Ed Teel put a steady stare upon Hampton. Hampton had just confessed that he really was a horsethief.

'It's with that other stuff on the desk,' Deming replied to Hampton. 'Why?'

Hampton smiled. 'Because it's going to disappear. It's probably going to be burned between tonight and the trial tomorrow. I reckon your identification papers will disappear too.'

Deming swore. 'Gawddammit, this is insane. I own two ranches, I employ ten fulltime riders. I know the governor of Wyoming personally, and any bank in Cheyenne will vouch for me.'

Hampton grinned at the older man's discomfort. 'I'll tell you something, Mister Deming: That would impress me, and I reckon it'd impress Ed, here, and a lot of other folks around Mandan—except that they aren't going to be allowed to hear it—but don't a word of that mean a thing to Abel Spencer, and he's the one we got to impress to stay alive.' Hampton looked out through the bars to the mound of Deming's personal possessions on the desk yonder. 'Meachem and Spencer'll burn that stuff sure as hell, and when you are arraigned along with me tomorrow, Mister Deming, you're going to be just another horse-stealin' cowboy on the run.'

The roadway door opened and Hampton swung his glance, expecting Henry Meachem. It was Hank Teel, bundled against the outside cold. He looked around the office as though unwilling to believe Meachem wasn't there. But after that sweeping search, he wasted no time crossing to the cell, unbuttoning his coat and shoving the guns through the bars for Hampton to take and pass swiftly to Hugh Deming, who shoved them beneath the straw-filled mattress on the bunk. Then Hank stepped back, visibly nervous, went to put his back to the stove and struggled to regain his normal composure as he said, 'I never figured I'd be this lucky. Where is he?'

'Went out to get supper for us about an hour ago,' Ed explained. 'He'll be back soon, unless he got side-tracked at the saloon.'

Hank accepted this and spoke, again, quickly. 'Listen; it's stopped snowing out, but that don't mean much because it's two feet deep on the flat, so after you bust out you can't go very far. But I been working on this all afternoon, so you listen now. Don't bust out until maybe after midnight tonight when everyone's asleep except whoever is guarding you in here. That way, folks won't know there's been a jailbreak until morning and by then...' Hank shrugged. 'Once you're out, come down to the shop, and don't use the front entrance, come in from the back alley.'

Hampton said, 'Tracks?'

'I got three of Ed's livery horses in my corral across the alley,' Hank explained. 'As soon as you fellers are down there and I've shown you where I figure you can hide, I'm going to ride up and down through the snow.'

Hampton nodded about this, and moved on to what occupied him next. 'You better leave, Hank. Meachem might not raise too much hell, you being in here when he comes back, but if we get out of here, come morning he's going to remember who came to visit us.'

Ed agreed with this. Hank had done all he'd hoped to accomplish anyway, so he left, and although the prisoners could hardly avoid looking and acting different now that there was new hope for them, Henry Meachem did not return for a full hour after Hank's departure, and by then his prisoners had resumed at least enough of an outward appearance of resignation and dejection to delude the new town marshal.

Deming made it seem even more natural by offering Meachem a thousand dollar bribe. The muddy-eyed range-rider was sitting over at Ed's desk when Deming made his offer, and he laughed. No doubt about it, before Meachem decided to return with the three tin plates for his prisoners, he had enjoyed a lengthy sojourn at the bar.

'Thousand dollars,' he sneeringly retorted, 'wouldn't even get me interested, mister, and you don't have it anyhow.'

Deming ate while still seated with his leg propped up. Between mouthfuls he said, 'I can get it within two days.'

Meachem's sneer deepened. 'How? By magic? No stages are going to get through to Mandan with no mail from Wyoming or anywhere else, for maybe a month; at least until the snow melts off the roadway.'

Deming did not give up. 'I can get it over in Craig. 'I've got friends over there. That's a lot closer than Wyoming.'

'No it ain't,' contradicted Meachem. 'When you're as snowed in as we are in Mandan, mister, Craig might just as well be on the moon.'

Meachem's answers were correct. Deming probably understood that as well as Ed Teel and Hampton did, but he kept trying. 'I'll give you something to think about,' he told Meachem. 'My word is good. If I say I'll pay you a thousand dollars. I'll pay it even if we have to wait a week or two before the mail can arrive here again. And Meachem, if you keep getting in deeper with that crazy judge up the road, you'd better think ahead, because even if he hangs the three of us, it isn't going to end there. When an investigation is made you're going to be just as guilty of murder as Spencer is.'

Meachem arose and went to get himself a cup of coffee at the stove. The three prisoners watched him closely, looking for some sign of wavering resolution, or apprehension. Meachem filled a cup and turned. He was smiling again.

'Boys, when Abe Spencer plans things won't no strangers come riding in to investigate things a month or two from now, that'll find anything but the graves of a couple of outlaws. Abe is a damned clever man.'

Ed said, 'A couple of graves?'

Meachem got the implication immediately and sipped coffee while he delayed his answer and while he stared with obvious dislike at Teel. 'Maybe *three* graves, Teel. If it was me, I'd damned well make it three, and not just so's you wouldn't be around to talk, but also because I hate your lousy guts. You been making trouble for range-riders who come to town for a little excitement ever since I been around the high meadow country. I'm not the only one who's got no use for you. Even some of the townsmen hate your guts.'

Hampton was leaning on the wall as he quietly said, 'You lousy bastard, Meachem. I wish I had a gun.'

The new town marshal reacted, at first, as he would have normally reacted, but that only lasted a moment, then he laughed with a booming sound. He did not respond with words, but sauntered back and sat behind the desk, holding his coffee cup in both hands, looking through the bars at Hampton with sadistic pleasure.

Hampton turned his back to the room and resumed his study of the ghostly dark night that was visible through his alley window. Meachem let the silence run on until he was willing to break it, then he said, 'Hey, Hampton, I already made arrangements with His Honour to buy that bay horse for thirty dollars—after you're swung up. Abe agreed because he figures it's going to take that much cash to get someone interested in grave-digging this time of year, with the damned ground froze down fifteen inches. Hampton; you ain't going to be sunk real deep. How does that sound to you?'

The black-eyed man did not speak, did not even look around. He had finished his plate of stew ahead of the other two prisoners, and remained with his back to everyone.

The night was clearing. An occasional star shone with frigid clarity through rifts in the broken clouds. The storm had passed. Now, the bitter cold would come. As soon as the sky got completely clear and the wind departed, the temperature would drop steadily and instead of a light crust of ice atop the snow, it would freeze down to a depth of perhaps six to eight inches—enough, perhaps, to support a man on a horse, but whether it froze down that far this first frigid night, or not, it would certainly freeze down deeply enough to support a man on snowshoes.

That was what Hampton thought as he stood gazing out the narrow, barred window. All he wanted now, was to get as far away from Mandan as he could possibly get, even if it meant abandoning his saddlebags, still hidden up in the aspen grove. Even if it meant risking his life by travelling without anything but a blanket and perhaps a tin or two of beans.

CHAPTER 13

Break-out!

Ed Teel asked Meachem to let them have the checkerboard inside the cell to while away time, and Meachem smiled and shook his head. 'Set and sweat,' he retorted. 'Teel, this is a time I been waiting for ever since the first time you locked me in for having a few too many. And I ain't the only one.'

Hugh Deming yawned, lifted his leg into a fresh position on the chair-seat, and looked impassively at Ed. Hampton saw the look and understood its significance. Teel acted as though he had not noticed. It was only a little past nine o'clock, and Hank had advised against breaking out before the town was bedded down, which was good advice, except that on a night like this one when it got dark by five o'clock, the town would be abed long before midnight.

Henry Meachem spent the time by going through Ed's desk, reading things he found filed there, and examining the guns and shell-

141

belts he had taken from his prisoners. He did not seem sleepy. As a matter of fact Ed knew that Meachem ordinarily spent half the night at the bar so he was not very hopeful about Meachem dozing off even though the jailhouse was a little warmer than Ed liked to keep it.

Hampton piled their supper tins one atop the other and used his boot-toe to shove them back under the door. Then he went to sit on the bunk beside Hugh Deming, and Ed Teel knew the other two prisoners were getting impatient. But when they gazed quizzically at him, Ed remained impassively non-committal.

A little before ten o'clock Abel Spencer arrived. Evidently this was a pre-arranged visit because Meachem was not the slightest bit surprised. He was lolling at the desk, coat off, hat propped back on his head, the half-empty bottle of whisky he had found in a lower desk drawer, on the desk in front of him. Spencer saw that first, even before he turned and glared at the prisoners. He shot Meachem a quick, probing look and the bully smiled indifferently as he said, 'Don't worry, Your Honour, I won't get smoked up. There ain't enough in the bottle to do that job anyway.'

Then, finally, Spencer turned towards the three seated men in the cell and fixed a bitter, strangely wild stare upon them. He seemed to

142

have relegated Hampton, his earlier fixation, a secondary place, because as he walked over and stood just out of reach beyond the bars, he looked squarely at Ed Teel.

'You asked for it,' he said in a bitter tone of voice. 'You been asking for it for a long while, Ed, what with overlookin' it when drunks got troublesome, and other derelictions of duty. Now, I got you as an accessory to horse-stealing.'

Ed stared steadily out at Abe Spencer, but he was past being surprised any more, so his look was antagonistic without being otherwise troubled. 'You're crazy,' he pronounced. 'Abe, you've gone to the end of your rope this trip. I had no idea you were this far gone.'

Spencer's face burned red. 'We'll see who's crazy, Ed. By gawd come morning we'll see who is wrong. I'm going to try you for being an accessory, for helping this damned pair of outlaws.'

'Helping them do what?' asked Ed, frowning.

'You conspired with them,' exclaimed Spencer. 'Don't deny it, damn you. You and Hampton didn't rescue this feller who claims to be the owner of the bay gelding. You snuck out of town with Hampton and made it look like you was trying to rescue someone, then you came back with this feller, you faked his broken leg, and the three of you conspired to make folks believe he's Deming and he give a bill-of-sale to Hampton. Ed, you're in this so deep you'll be lucky when I present the evidence tomorrow for everyone to hear, if they don't meet in the saloon and make up a lynch-party.'

'Which,' said Deming to Abe Spencer, 'is exactly what you're aiming for, isn't it, Spencer?' The rancher's expression showed purest contempt. 'If you are the judge you can't present evidence. You can't prosecute. Don't you know any more law than that? You are only supposed to sit in judgement, to be impartial and to make your judgement based on what is proven, according to legal precedents governing the hearing—and *not* the trial—the hearing. Spencer, you're putting your damned neck on the block, acting like this.'

For a moment Abel Spencer glared, then he swung and said, 'Henry, you watch. If that one tries to escape, shoot him.'

Meachem nodded, but he showed some puzzlement. 'He couldn't get out, Judge, not with his busted leg in splints. I don't see how any of them could get out anyway, that cell—'

'I said, Henry, you watch close. And that man's no more got a broken leg then I have. Did you check inside those wrappings, Henry?

144

He could have a gun cached in there.'

Meachem's quick, small mind turned this idea over several times before he arose behind the desk, hitched up his shellbelt and stepped round front. 'I didn't think of that,' he said, as Abe Spencer stepped to the roadway door. 'He just damned well might have a gun hid inside the bandaging at that.'

Hampton saw Meachem's sadistic smile coming. He knew exactly what Abe Spencer had done—planted the idea in Meachem's mind that he could legally kill the prisoners. He also thought he knew why Spencer had done that; because his overpowering hatred for at least two of them, Hampton and Deming, whom he was convinced were outlaws, drove him to want those two killed, and of course he wouldn't have to tell Meachem that a survivor, a living witness with friends around town—Ed Teel— should never be left to point an accusing finger. As far as Hampton was concerned, midnight could damned well be too late.

Spencer left the jailhouse but Henry Meachem remained leaning on the front of the desk, smiling into the cell without saying a word until Ed spoke first, saying, 'Henry, if you let Abe talk you into murder, believe me, you'll hang sure as I'm sitting here.'

Meachem hated Teel. The other two were

not really important to him one way or the other; because he put no value on life, though, they were in almost as much danger as Ed was. The difference was that Meachem was looking forward to shooting Ed Teel, was concentrating on that to the exclusion of much else, so, if he could, he most certainly would commit that particular murder; the other murders he would also commit, but with detachment because neither Hampton nor Deming meant anything to Meachem.

'You go right ahead and whine a little,' he told Ed. 'You beg a little, Teel, and maybe I'll listen—and maybe I won't listen.'

Hampton leaned back on the wall-bunk with a hand behind him. Hugh Deming's proximity hid Hampton's unseen arm, but from the corner of his eye Ed Teel saw and understood. Clearly, Hampton figured Meachem was going to start shooting at any moment now. Ed, who knew Meachem, did not believe it was going to happen this soon, but he could hardly tell Hampton not to pull out the gun, so he made a final desperate bid to divert Meachem by arising and stepping over to the bars. 'Even if we're isolated, Henry, and no one can get through for another week or so, all that will do is postpone trouble for you, if you do what Abe hinted at.'

Meachem's smile faded. 'That ain't begging, Teel. I want to hear you really whine and cry.'

Hampton arose and strolled forward to stand slightly to one side of Ed at the bars. Hampton had both hands behind him, as though they were in his rear trouser pockets. 'Anybody who'd beg to a worthless bastard like you,' he said quietly, looking straight at Meachem, 'would have to be a lot more scairt than I think any of us are.'

This was the second time Hampton had called Meachem that fighting name. The first time it had stung, but Meachem had laughed it off. This time he did not laugh, he straightened up off the desk with both hands hanging at his sides, the right hand within inches of his hip-holstered sidearm. 'Mister, I'm going to kill you for that,' he told Hampton. 'You been asking for it ever since I locked you there. Now, I'm goin' to see you get it.'

Hampton brought his right hand forward and cocked the sixgun as he steadied it on Meachem, through the bars. 'Draw,' he said. 'Meachem, draw!'

There was no question about Meachem's intentions, even if he hadn't been dumbfounded at sight of the gun. Behind Hampton, from back on the wall-bunk, Hugh Deming was also

147

pointing a sixgun. Without taking his eyes off Meachem he held out a third weapon, butt-first, to Ed, who took it and examined the cylinder before he shoved the weapon into his waistband.

Meachem was scarcely breathing. In a matter of seconds his position had been completely reversed, and Hampton did not appear to be the kind that Meachem was, Hampton was not a man who prolonged a killing, it showed very clearly in his face that he would pull the trigger within moments. Meachem leaned back with both hands gripping the edge of the desk behind him.

'Don't shoot,' he croaked. 'Listen, Hampton, I was just tryin' to scare you. Hones' to gawd that's what I was doing.'

Deming, like Ed Teel, had lowered his own weapon to allow Hampton the full initiative. All Deming did was give Meachem an order. 'Pick that gun out of your hoster, and let it drop. Don't even look down at it!'

Meachem was willing but he looked first at Hampton; *that* was where his immediate destiny would be decided. Hampton nodded his head, and Henry Meachem disarmed himself. With his gun went whatever vestiges of courage he had retained.

'The key,' said Hampton, leaning casually

148

on the bars.

Meachem twisted and felt atop Ed's desk until he found it. He leaned to offer the key to Ed but Hampton said, 'Unlock it yourself, Meachem. Hurry up at it!'

Meachem apprpoached the cell as though he were approaching a firing squad. There was fresh sweat on his face and his movements were stiffly awkward. When he unlocked the door and swung it back, he raised pleading eyes. It was wasted effort. Hampton gestured for Meachem to enter the cell. When he hesitated, Ed caught him by the arm and wrenched him forward. As Ed let go, as Meachem sought to whirl and spring sideways, Deming shoved his good leg and Meachem tripped and started down. That was when Hampton swung. He caught Meachem on the back of the head with his pistol barrel. The falling man gave a spasmodic lunge, throwing out both arms, then he struck the floor and half rolled just once, as limp as a rag.

Hampton smiled at Deming. 'Thanks for the trip.'

Deming grinned back. 'Any time.' He jockeyed forward on the bunk to arise, and Hamptpon offered his free hand. Deming used the hand to arise, then he said, 'You boys go on. There is no damned sense at all in me slow-ing you down. A man with a broken leg is about as useful in an escape as a log-chain necklace twenty feet long.'

'Escape where,' snapped Teel. 'You can hop, as far as my brother's blacksmith shop, and I don't see any of us going a hell of a lot farther, not in two or three feet of freezing snow. A man can't travel ten yards in that without stopping to suck air.'

Hampton went to the door and looked out. The town was still huddled and only indifferently lighted. Along the main thoroughfare only the gunshop and the saloon had bright windows, every other storefront was dark. Undoubtedly, out back where most residences were, people were still up, but no one was outside on the plankwalks, and that was what Hampton needed to ascertain before he opened the door wider and jerked his head. As Ed helped Deming forward, Hampton stepped to the desk, dug out three shellbelts with holstered guns, slung them from his shoulder, then he went over and locked the unconscious town marshal inside the cell. He called Meachem that name again, then turned and slipped out into the freezing night and locked the door after himself.

Ed and Hugh Deming were making slow progress in the direction of the liverybarn, and beyond it, towards the blacksmith shop. Hampton hurried along to lend ahand with Deming from the opposite side. No one said anything. Their boots crunching over frosty snow and forming ice made echoes in the night that sounded as loud and revealing to Hampton as pistol shots. But when he looked back the town had not changed; there still was no one outside in the roadway.

Ed hoped his brother would be ready. 'We weren't supposed to break out for another couple of hours.'

Deming answered that through clenched teeth. 'Yeah? And if we'd waited that long, Teel, I don't think we'd have needed to have a break out. He was going to kill the three of us sure as all hell.'

No one argued about that, and within moments of it being said, Hank appeared, evidently alerted to their arrival by the sounds they made walking through ice and snow.

CHAPTER 14

Hideout!

The front of Hank's blacksmithing shop was closed, and for once that big old sagging front door that stuck served a good purpose; it fit so snugly that no light reached the roadway beyond it.

The shop was warm and Hank seemed relieved, not upset, that the escapees had arrived early. Evidently the long wait had been harder on him than it had been on them.

He had coffee heating. They had a cup, all around, then Hank, frankly nervous although it was improbable that anyone would find the unconscious man in the jailhouse for hours yet to come, led the way out into the bitter night. He took them to a ladder alongside his shop that had evidently not been in place long, and told them that as soon as they were all in the low loft above his shop he would take away the ladder. Hampton and Deming thought nothing much of what they had to do—get one-legged Hugh Deming up there—but Ed frowned as he gazed upwards. 'Are you plumb sure there's enough room for three men?' he asked. 'I didn't know you had a loft to the shop, Hank. It always looked to me as though the ceiling inside went all the way up.'

Hank motioned for his brother to climb first. 'I hope everyone else figures the same way,' he said. 'Hurry up, will you? There's enough room up there without any to spare. I put some stuff up there for you fellers to eat. Also flung up some blankets, and I'll have to keep the forge going or you'll freeze.' Hank paused and watched his brother go up the ladder. 'And lie real still once you're comfortable,' he called softly, 'because the damned building creaks real easy, and sure as hell Abe'll come talk to me.'

Hampton, with no great love for confined places even when they might save his life, helped Deming start up, then he turned towards Hank with a grave expression. 'If anyone thinks of your attic they won't have to find the outside crawl-hole—they can just cut loose with a few rounds from down inside the shop.'

Hank was impatient and that made him irritable. 'Yeah, and the damned roof could cave in from snow, too, but I don't expect that to happen either. Now get the hell up there, will you?'

Hampton got. He had his head and shoulders through the opening when down below Hank moved to take away the ladder. Hampton turned to say something about a candle, but Hank held a hand up for silence. Up the road someone let out a yell.

Hampton wriggled into the attic, turned back to close the crawl-hole gently and quietly, and down below Hank made haste with the ladder. He took it to the back of his shop and bent low to shove it under the sagging old rear porch. Then he ran to do as he had previously planned to do, wipe out those tell-tale tracks.

In the utterly black attic, although it was surprisingly and pleasantly warm from the rising heat, Hampton could only make out the faces of his companions when one of them said something and he faced in that direction. Even then, faces were simply pale ovals.

Ed worried about that yell. He thought it had originated at the jailhouse. Hampton did not dispute this, but it had seemed to him to originate farther up the road and over on the far side, and Hampton had still been partly out of the attic when the yell had come, while Ed had been deep inside.

Deming worried about the tracks they had left. 'Three men,' he said, 'showing five boot-tracks. They won't have to be very smart to

154

figure that out, will they? And if we're caught up here it's not going to be very heroic; be like cornered rats.' He moved a little, making his aching leg comfortable. Hank had confiscated horseblankets from his brother's liverybarn for the men in the attic hidehout. No one had to *see* that this was so, their noses told them. After Deming had settled his injured leg, had got comfortable in a half-prone, half-propped, position, he lay like his companions, listening.

There had been no second yell from the roadway, but if a crowd of men were inside the jailhouse there probably would be no second yell anyway. Hank, of course, could eventually have explained what that noise had been about, but Hank was too busy tramping out tracks. Hampton learned the first lesson of an escapee: suspense. He drew his gun and examined it almost entirely by feel. The second gun, the one sticking in his waistband, was uncomfortable when he sat or squatted, so he removed it, placed it where he thought he'd be able to find it again in the dark if he had to, and tried to see what Ed was up to when Teel began inching forward.

The attic was much too low for any of them to sit up but they could do as Deming was doing, they could lie on one side and prop them-

155

selves up by one arm. Ed crawled to the front of the buildling and searched for a crack that would allow him to see the roadway. There were several cracks, all caused by the warping and weathering of the wood, but they provided only a very limited view of the roadway directly in front of the shop, and with no moon and only distant, brittle little stars to give light even that view was rather negative.

Ed wriggled back and reported. 'Can't see up or down the road, but it's too quiet out there. If they'd discovered Meachem, believe me, there would be some kind of noise.'

Hampton was not quite convinced of this, but for the time being he was not too anxious. If Hank had succeeded in destroying the tracks from the jailhouse, even though Spencer would know the fugitives had to still be in town some-where, it would require a little time to organize searching parties. What bothered him most was that Hank was the first person Spencer would suspect. He told the others searchers would go over the liverybarn and the shoeing shop board by board.

Neither Teel nor Deming refuted this, but Deming said, 'If we'd been unable to break out, Meachem would have shot us by now and claimed we were trying to escape. At least we're still alive.' Then Deming growled resentment against his broken leg. 'I'd trade a lot of horses right this minute not to have this injury. For once, I wish to hell Spencer had been right about me faking it.' He lay back and the boards squeaked under his weight. 'It crossed my mind this evening that being a good samaritan can get folks killed.' Deming said this so dryly Hampton smiled in the darkness.

'Hey, Ed,' he murmured. 'You were plumb right, I'm a horsethief.'

Teel acknowledged this without much show of feeling. 'Yeah, I know.'

'Well; when you first locked me up you weren't so sure.'

Teel still showed no feeling. 'It wasn't that I don't believe you were—or weren't—Hampton, it was just that I was beginning to have some second thoughts about what was going to happen. Like I already told you, folks made one bad mistake in lynching a feller here, once, and right or wrong, I made up my mind long ago there were not going to be any more of those whisky-barrel judgements handed down as long as I was town marshal.'

Hampton said, 'And now? You're not the law, Spencer is.'

'What of it,' responded Teel. 'I'm still opposed to lynch-law.'

Deming sounded roughly amused by this as

157

he said, 'Nice point of law, Teel. I'll remember it as they adjust the ropes for all three of us.' Then Deming made the board beneath his pallet squeak again as he rolled up on to one side and propped his head on one palm. 'They'll find us up here sooner or later. Seems to me we've got to try and figure a better hiding place.'

Down below in the shop someone worked the forge-treadle. It made a growling sound as wind was forced up through the clinkers and coal and oak knots. That would be Hank, and if he was back inside, it meant he had finished destroying their tracks.

Hampton did not think much of this. 'Your brother being in his shop this late at night will look suspicious,' he told Ed. 'No one shoes horses at midnight.'

Ed got no chance to reply. From below a hammer striking steel made harsh music. Obviously, Hank was just as aware of what Hampton had thought as the others were, and had gone to work down there. To Hampton, it still looked like a mistake. He did not believe the blacksmith should have remained in the shop at all.

But an hour later when the hammering stopped, there had been no interruption, so perhaps, whatever that yell had signified, did not mean that Meachem had been found.

They heard Hank leave by the sticking front door, and not very long afterwards they also noticed that the heat was yielding to the creeping cold. The worst part of this kind of hiding was that there was no way to know what was going on down below, or up at the saloon where Spencer and his townsmen would be spending their time in comfort.

Ed thought that if that yell had no significance, most of the men in the saloon would shortly be heading for home and bed, and he was correct, but when Deming offered to stay awake and act as their sentinel, Ed told Deming and Hampton to rest, that he would keep a vigil up from where the cracks would allow him to watch the roadway. Deming, who seemed to be a man of no nerves, or else very strong ones, sighed and lay back. Of the three fugitives, he had suffered most in the escape. Just climbing that ladder had exhausted him. Of all the endeavours a one-legged man could undertake, ladder-climbing had to be just about the most exacting.

Hampton lay back, too, but he did not close his eyes. He was groping in his mind for some better way out of their predicament than lying like torpid snakes in a sooty attic above a blacksmith shop. But every alternative that came

159

along ended when he thought of the snow-bound condition of the entire town.

The odds favoured Abel Spencer and the men he could whip into excited—and mindless —action, as soon as Meachem was discovered locked in the jailhouse. If it had been possible to leave town, Hampton thought the three of them might have some chance. He had learned the value of movement, of covering miles of land at the same time he had avoided people and ranches and towns. Even if they'd had to use a buggy, because of Deming's injury, they still might have a chance. But being snow-bound in Mandan with half or perhaps two-thirds of the town against them with guns and ropes and lanterns, he did not believe any attic or even any root-celler, would save them from eventual discovery.

Spencer was insane, Hampton was convinced of that, but he was not unreasonably crazy; he would launch a search, come morning, that would leave the town thoroughly searched.

Ed Teel turned, from over near the front wall, and said, 'You awake, Hampton?'

'Yeah.'

'Why did you steal the bay horse?'

'I told you, Ed. I didn't have enough money to buy him. To buy any horse.'

Teel's comment about that showed how his

thoughts were running. 'A man can cut wood this time of year, or he can get a temporary job stacking hay. There are jobs in the towns if a man needs money.'

All this was true. 'Wait,' said Hampton. 'Wait until they've got us with our hands tied in back, then I'll tell you the whole story.'

From over in the darkness where Deming was supposedly sleeping a quiet voice said, 'Why wait, cowboy? They're not going to hang us now, they are going to shoot us on sight... Go ahead, tell him about Montana.'

Hampton glanced over where Deming was and made out only a lumpy shape. 'That must have been quite a telegram you got over in Craig,' he said.

Deming answered indifferently. 'It was. After all—Walter Nelson—you've been about a month on the trail. All the law ever needed was some idea of your whereabouts. They had already begun to track you by the stolen horses.'

Ed Teel, listening to this exchange, twisted away from the building-front to listen as Hampton spoke again. 'If you knew all this, Deming, why did you try and save me with that lie about the bill-of-sale, this morning?'

'Funny thing,' drawled Hugh Deming from the darkness, 'but no matter who you were, cowboy, you saved my life. Maybe something like that isn't too damned important to folks around Mandan, but it is to me.'

'So you'd have let met get away?' asked Hampton, and Deming answered in the same calm drawl.

'No. I couldn't have done that, cowboy, but I figured out a way that wouldn't bother my conscience if you did get away, and at the same time I'd have repaid the debt I owed you.'

Hampton was baffled. 'How?'

'Easy,' said Deming. 'Give it back. I'd see it went up to those folks who own it. *Then* you could ride away.'

CHAPTER 15

Restless Fugitives

From over where he had been listening, Ed Teel said, 'Give *what* back, Deming?'

The rancher's answer was commensurate with Deming's character. 'Ask your horsethief, Teel, it's his story.'

Ed obeyed. 'Hampton...?'

It probably did not matter anyway, now that there was no way out of Mandan, and that by morning searchers would be swarming all over town looking for him, but Hampton was still inhibited. Not entirely because, until now, this had been his secret, but also because it seemed that a revelation was the same as giving up his dream. On the other hand, Deming was correct, the three of them were going to be shot on sight. They had barely escaped death inside the jailhouse, when they had made no attempt to escape. Now, they were escapees, fugitives from the law, and Abel Spencer, Henry Meachem, anyone else Spencer could whip into a killing mood, would shoot the three of them to death on sight, and be justified. That was pure range-law.

Deming, waiting in the darkness, said, 'Cowboy, where you are going you can't spend a cent of it. Why not tell him?'

Hampton raised up in the darkness looking in Ed's direction. 'I robbed a bank at Pine Falls, Montana, and got twenty-five thousand dollars.' Neither Teel nor Deming made a sound. Deming already knew, so he lay in ironic silence, but Ed Teel's silence was completely different.

'I planned it for a year,' Hampton explained. 'I read all about the successful and the unsuccessful bank robbers. Then I planned it to be near fool-proof. I even figured in the weather so's no posse could catch me, and I stole fresh horses out of pastures and off the range, and never let anyone catch sight of me—if I could help it. Right up until I stole Deming's bay horse, I was winning. He was the best riding animal, and partner, I ever had. When he got tenderfoot I should have abandoned him and stolen a fresh one, but no, I got sentimental and rode into Mandan to have him shod. You and Hank know the rest of the story, Ed.'

Teel's astonishment had passed by this time. 'Where is the twenty-five thousand dollars, Hampton?'

'Hidden. If things get bad I'll tell you where it is. No point in nobody getting the use of it.'

Deming spoke. 'That's why I brought it up, cowboy. Things *are* bad. They might get worse, but if they do, take my word for it, you're not going to have time enough to tell anyone where the money is. What's the use of letting it rot somewhere after you're dead?'

It was not as easy for Hampton to make this kind of a decision as it was for Hugh Deming, or Ed Teel, to make it. He considered that stolen fortune his personal property, his own private wealth. He had only taken it because he had spent his lifetime at hard, often dangerous, physical labour, and had looked ahead, had seen himself continuing to spend his life that way until he was too old, or too crippled, to go on doing it, then he knew what happened to his kind because every saloon and liverybarn had broken down rangeriders emptying the spittoons, dunging out the stalls, sleeping in smelly little harness rooms or cubbyholes behind bar-rooms.

'Maybe later,' he said, and lay back. 'Deming, you're an owner. I'll tell you something: I don't hold it against a man that he's smarter than I've been, or that opportunities came along and he made something of them that I was maybe too dumb to see and do anything

165

about. But you got to understand how it is with me: Damned if I'm going to end up drinking myself to sleep every night because I'm too old or stiffed-up to hold a saddle-backing job, and this is my way out. I know—it's wrong—that's what you and Teel will say. I wouldn't argue that with you. *I* know it's wrong. But that doesn't change anything for me, does it, except that it increases the risks. Well, I'm willing to take those chances. I also know that if everyone looked at things like I do, there'd be busted banks all over the country. But everyone *doesn't*, do they?'

Ed Teel did not see the match-flare but he smelled the smoke when Hampton lit up. 'Suppose,' he said, 'you say where the money is, Hampton, and if any of us come out of this alive—'

'Supppose *all* of us come out of it alive,' interrupted Hampton, hitting at the crux of Ed's suggestion. 'Then where are we?'

Hugh Deming sounded as though he were yawning when he answered. 'I hope we all do, cowboy, but the point Teel was about to make, I think, is that if you say where the damned money is, then at least the chances are three-to-one that someone will be able to see that it's returned. If you're the only one who knows where it is, and you get killed, it'll

166

probably be lost forever. I don't figure you to be that cold-hearted a bank robber.'

There was another alternative. 'I'll tell you where it is,' agreed Hampton, 'providing I have the word of both of you that if I live through this mess neither of you'll try to stop me or try to get the money when I get a chance to ride on. If I don't make it, then suit yourselves; keep it or give it back.'

Deming did not even hesitate to answer, but Ed did. Deming was an honest man, but not a very complicated one. He said, 'Agreed. If they kill you and I survive, which is as unlikely as hell, the money goes back to Montana. Teel...?'

Ed hadn't quite decided yet, but there was one influencing factor: No matter how moral he wanted to be, there was one hell of a small chance of him living past tomorrow. 'I'll agree,' he told Hampton, 'only to let you ride off. I won't agree not to try and catch you with the money afterwards.'

Hampton smiled and the other men saw his teeth in the gloom. 'Ed, you couldn't catch me if I had Deming's busted leg, but that's for you to find out later. All right. The money is in my saddlebags tied high in one of the trees in that aspen grove up the north road from Mandan. You know that grove, Ed?'

Teel knew it. He had reason to know it; it had been up there that his predecessor and the lynch-crowd hanged that settler for allegedly stealing beef. 'I know the place. I hope you tied those saddlebags solid.'

Hampton had few doubts on that score but he did not say so because now he felt as though he had somehow just given away his fortune; had at least made it more improbable than ever that he would be able to recover it, alone.

Deming, who had been quiet for a while, now said, 'Everybody has hard times, cowboy. I didn't stumble into a cave full of bullion to get my start. But even if I had, damned if I can understand why you'd want to break a lot of folks who've been saving their pennies and putting them in a bank, and you didn't even know those folks.'

For Hampton, because he was not a man given to delusions, there had never been a real justification, except that very elemental one that involved old age, being crippled, being alone and destitute and helpless, so when he replied to Hugh Deming he was completely honest.

'I reckon your telegram didn't give all the details after all, Deming. I didn't rob but four accounts, and every one was someone like you, that I knew had the money. I wasn't trying to be a damned Robin Hood, I just didn't want

168

to wake up nights thinking about those people you mentioned, the ones who saved pennies. The other ones, well, I knew every one of them. I'd worked for two of them. They wouldn't get demoralized, they'd raise hell and grab guns and try to find me. That was how I wanted it to be. I figured I was better at running and cutting back and leaving false trails, and out-smarting them on the run, than they'd be at overtaking me, but I also figured if they *did* catch me—then I'd take whatever they handed out, and that would be that.'

Deming sighed. 'Okay,' he said quietly. 'You want me to sum it up for you? There was never a loner, cowboy, who couldn't be run down—providing folks knew that he had a weakness. Every loner has one. Yours was the bay horse. Maybe it's your substitute for a family. Anyway, here you are, and win, lose, or draw, I'll make a bet with you. You don't ride out of Mandan with that damned money.'

Hampton said in a flat tone, 'You figure to stop me?'

Deming answered in his customary calm voice. 'Nope. I'm not even going to try to stop you.' He paused, and when Ed and Hampton expected him to explain, he changed the subject by saying. 'Why don't we figure something better than lying up here waiting to be flushed out? This was all right to start with, but the forge-fire's dying and if we don't freeze solid by morning, we're going to get caught anyway. Teel; you know the town. Where can three men lie low without being found?'

Ed already knew the answer to that. 'Nowhere. Not if Spencer organizes a real hunt for us.'

Deming grunted about that, then made a suggestion that seemed, at least for a moment, to have merit. 'All right. Suppose we can get those snowshoes you boys had when you rescued me; how far out to the first ranch, or to some shack or hut where we'd at least be able to stand up like men and see them coming?'

Hampton said, 'You can't make it on snowshoes, Deming.'

The rancher had his answer ready. 'Maybe not, but I've sure got one hell of an incentive to *try*.'

Hampton did not think much of this kind of talk. 'We'd still leave tracks in the snow— even if you could make it with Ed and me.'

Deming reverted to his earlier statement. 'I'd prefer taking my chances standing up like a man than lying in here like a rat.'

While Deming and Hampton argued, Ed Teel had a thought. It did not offer much hope for escape, but it had elements of a kind of salvation in it. 'Listen, you two. Instead of running, which Spencer's going to figure we'll do, suppose we get down out of here now—at two o'clock in the morning when not a soul's stirring—and go visit Abel.'

Hampton and Deming twisted in darkness to stare over where Teel squatted near the front wall. They both caught the implication immediately. Perhaps something like this should have occurred to someone before this, and no doubt the reason it hadn't occurred to them was because they had been thinking in terms of flight, of hiding, of escape. This wasn't *de*fence, this was *of*fence.

Deming seemed to agree when he said, 'This gawddamned leg.'

Hampton, the practical, pragmatic outlaw, blew out a big breath then said, 'You've a pretty good head, Marshal. All right. But after we have him—what?'

'Hostage,' said Deming.

Hampton already knew this. 'Sure; but we're still snowbound aren't we?'

The only thing they could do, and Ed said as much, was try for as much time as possible. If they could gain another day that was better than waiting to be killed. They had already cheated death once, and now they had an opportunity to perhaps cheat it again. 'We're playing for hours at a time,' he told the other two men. 'That's all we can do. Sooner or later the town's going to find us, up here or down at Spencer's building, it's too small a town for things to work out otherwise for us. But maybe, if we have a hostage, we can hang on for another day, and that's the best we can hope for right now, isn't it?'

Deming thought so. 'I'm willing. But there's one problem—how the hell do we get down out of here?'

That brought Hampton back into the discussion. 'I can drop down into the snow and find that damned ladder.' He turned as though this were already agreed upon, and crawled over to ease open the weathered little crawl-hole door. At once, frigid night air rushed in to dispel the little heat remaining in their stuffy hiding place. Also, starlight, reflecting upwards from the sparkling snow brought enough light in for them to see one another better.

Deming, watching as Hampton squirmed around to drop feet first, said, 'Bend your knees and roll. What we *don't* need is another busted leg.'

Hampton eased down until he was hanging by the fingers, then dropped. The height was not great and the snow, even with its inch-thick ice coating, acted as a two-foot-deep cushion.

When Ed crawled over and peered out, Hampton was getting to his feet and shaking the snow off. He did not look up to wave that he was all right, he went swiftly towards the back of the shop, and from the pale-lighted gloom behind Teel, the rancher said, 'Marshal, I sure hope to hell I've got that man figured right.'

Ed looked over his shoulder. 'Meaning what?'

'That we are still up here, and he's down there, and he's a good man on snowshoes, and maybe that aspen grove isn't so far he couldn't reach it and be on his way with about four or five hours head-start before morning.'

Ed stared at Hugh Deming. Somewhere over on the east side of town a dog started barking. He may have heard something, or he may have caught the scent of a shrunken-gutted prowling wolf.

CHAPTER 16

The First Hostage

The idea of trying to reach the aspen grove did not enter Hampton's considerations. He was searching for a ladder and until he found one he was like a bloodhound on a hot trail.

Perhaps if he'd taken the time to read sign he would have located the ladder Hank had shoved under his rear porch, but the ladder he eventually carried back to the south side of the blacksmith shop had been hanging in plain sight upon pegs next door at the liverybarn, and the point was not where a ladder came from nor to whom it belonged, the point was that when he eased it up against the shed and waited for Teel to help Hugh Deming back out of the attic and start downward, the ladder provided all three of them with a means for bridging the past, or what they had been able to do so far, with the future, or what they now sought to accomplish.

Deming of course was a hindrance and he knew it. When Hampton was removing the ladder after they were all on the ground again, he urged the others to let him stay behind because otherwise, if they had to run for it, he would be a dead weight.

Hampton smiled at the cowman. 'It'd help if you had two good legs,' he said, 'but what we're likely to need is a third gun. Anyway, we aren't likely to have to run any foot races for a week or so, until the snow melts. Let's go.'

They all knew where Spencer's building was but only Ed knew where Abel Spencer bedded down, up there. It was not a long walk, ordinarily, but tonight it was. They had to support Deming between them, and although Hank had previously trampled the alleyway snow to obscure their tracks, he had not done this north of the jailhouse, and neither had anyone else so the snow was deep and there were a number of bad drifts nearly blocking the upper end of the alleyway from the lower end.

Until now, they had thought very little about Henry Meachem, but they had progressed up the alley only a short distance past Ed's liverybarn when they saw the light up there. Someone was moving inside the building. In fact, it looked like several people because when a body moved across in front of the lamp, it was not always the same height or width.

Hampton began to wish they were back in the attic. Teel may have wished the same thing because he looked over his shoulder once, just as Hugh Deming said, 'I figured they'd rouse the town when they found Meachem. Rouse the town and organize search parties complete with torches and hangropes.'

Hampton gave a tough, and quite probably correct, explanation. 'They know we're in town and they also know we're going to still be in town come morning. When you know an animal is in your trap, you don't rush him because you know damned well he's got nothing to lose so he's going to fight as hard as he can. They know we're out here and they know we got guns.'

Ed Teel wondered aloud if Spencer were in the jailhouse, with those other men. It was quite probable, since Spencer was the leader. Hampton thought of this only in terms of deriving benefit.

'If he is, so much the better. That'll give us time to get up yonder to his building and be hiding in place when he returns.'

They resumed their trek, carefully and slowly because at any moment some enterprising Spencer-partisan might come ploughing through the snow alongside the jailhouse to walk out back. It was not too probable, but it *could* happen. All that the fugitives did *not* need right now was to be caught out in the open, backgrounded by snow and with no way of running to escape unless they abandoned Deming, which they would not do.

The activity inside the jailhouse, however, did not appear to be something that had begun very recently. Perhaps Meachem had been discovered, and liberated, a half hour or so earlier. To Hampton it seemed that whatever was in progress in there was being carried forward without any excitement, and that supported his view that Meachem had not just been discovered with a lump on his head, locked in the cell. It also encouraged him to think that if there had been any earlier explorations seeking the fugitives' tracks, those things had occurred long ago.

Deming was worried. 'They aren't waiting for morning. Give the devil his due, Spencer is organizing his search parties so quietly he probably figures we won't know what's going on until we're looking down someone's gunbarrel.'

They kept on going, reached the area immediately behind the jailhouse and did not stop again until they were on past. The cold was bitter enough to make their faces tingle, and their

177

breath to turn white in the starshine. It went through their clothing in a slow and paralysing way. If they'd had to spend many hours out of doors on this night they would have suffered, particularly, because up until recently they had been comfortably warm.

Movement helped. With Deming doing all he could to alleviate the burden for Teel and Hampton, they tramped across a three-foot drift and paused to blow on the far side, then went on again, the only sound anywhere around being made by their booted feet each time they crunched through the ice-layer with a fresh step. Silence was preferable but there was nothing to be done about that. Moreover, since it was so late at night by now, or so early in the morning, whichever way a person chose to view the time, no one was stirring among the houses and stores they went past.

They paused up near the north end of the alley to catch their breath and look back. It was no longer possible to see reflectd light from the jailhouse. In fact there was no light anywhere, except that weak and ghostly brightness that came dully off the snow.

Ed pointed ahead, up where a palisaded log wall stood. That was the boundary of the stageline's corral yard. He took them unerringly down the east side of the fence to its juncture with the front roadway, where the gate was.

This was the first good view they'd had of the main part of town since escaping. It showed a darkened town, except southward where jail-house-light fell outward to the roadway, but what Ed sought, and failed to find, was other men somewhere in sight. Satisfied, he took Deming and Hampton around into the yard and half-way across it in the direction of the stage-line office, which was downstairs, and the dark upstairs, which was the only local hostelry. They almost made it.

Hampton was on Deming's left and saw the bulky silhouette only after he had detected the tobacco smoke. He stopped in his tracks, forcing his companions to do the same. Evidently Abel Spencer kept a nighthawk on duty in his corral yard. If the man had been part of a more recently activated posse or search party he probably would have had a rifle or at least a carbine. As far as Hampton could make out, the man had neither, although he undoubtedly had a sixgun belted round his middle beneath the big sheep-pelt-lined coat he wore. He also wore heavy lined gloves and had his hat pulled down and his collar turned up. There was no way for Spencer's corral-yard-guard to get at his Colt before he could be surprised. Also, he was leaning in an attitude of either drowsiness or cold-stiffness upon the rear door of Spencer's building, beyond which was the local courtroom, which was recessed and therefore somewhat protected, with a cup of something hot, probably black coffee, in one gloved fist. He had his back to the fugitives; he appeared to be gazing northward but it was difficult to be sure of this.

Hampton disengaged himself from Deming, swept back his coat and drew his sixgun. The snow had been shovelled out of the gateway entrance to the yard, but where it had been flung made a high burm that was frozen on top. The minute Hampton sought to cross that piled snow to get closer, the guard would hear him coming.

Teel and Deming said nothing. There was no point in offering a warning anyway, Hampton knew his chances of success as well as they did. He stepped ahead, to the edge of the snow pile, raised his gun until starshine shone off it, looked around to be sure there was no second or third guard, then raised his voice to carry just as far as that bulky silhouette, and said, 'You want someone to spell you off?'

The guard turned quickly, but without acting alarmed until he saw the gun aimed at him. He looked over it to Hampton's face. A steamy big breath showed when he exhaled sharply. It took the man several seconds to assess his predicament. There was no way for him to resist, and stay alive.

Deming and Teel came forward, and as the guard's glance saw them too, he appeared to loosen a little as though he recognized the futility of whatever he might have had in mind.

Hampton gave the man an order that was obeyed to the letter. 'Don't move, mister. Keep facing me and don't move.' This was Teel's cue, he assisted Hugh Deming over and through the snow-bank as Hampton moved sideways so he'd have the nighthawk in his sights while the other two reached him. Deming leaned on the building, shivering, his broken leg held off the ground, while Ed Teel went over and looked closely at the nighthawk, then said, 'Hello, Frank. Is Abel inside?'

The guard shook his head without finding his voice for a moment. 'No. Marshal, you'd better get the hell away from here.'

Ed opened the man's coat and lifted away his holstered sidearm, then he stepped past and tried the door. It was not locked and yielded easily when Ed opened it. Warmth came from the interior blackness and with it the pleasant scent of wood-ash in a hot iron stove.

Hampton crossed the snow-pile as Teel went to assist Deming into the hushed and dark building. He and the guard exchanged a look, then Hampton prodded the man with his weapon. 'Follow the others,' he ordered. The nighthawk dutifully turned and went inside. Hampton left the door open because that was the only source of light. He had been in this room before and remembered it very well, but that other time it had been full of spectators and Abel Spencer had been sitting up at the judge's table.

The guard recovered from his shock and faced Teel. 'They're going to find you fellers no matter where you hide, Marshal. They got squads of men looking already, I think.'

Ed doubted this but he had no illusions; searchers might not be abroad yet, but they would be very shortly. 'How long has Abel been gone?' he asked. The nighthawk answered forthrightly.

'Fifteen minutes, I reckon. Couple of Henry's friends went down to take him a bottle and found him locked in and knocked over the head. One of 'em come up here and told Mister Spencer. Marshal, you ain't got a chance.'

Hampton interrupted. 'Shed your coat,' he said to the guard, 'and your hat.' To Deming and Teel he explained. 'Spencer'll be expecting his nighthawk to be outside. We wouldn't want to disappoint him, would we?'

The guard handed over his coat and hat and Hampton put them on. It was Deming who wondered aloud if Abel Spencer might not return with other men. Hampton had already thought of that.

'I'm not going to stand by the door, I'm going to be off a little ways near one of those parked stages. If he's alone I'll march him in here. If he's not alone—then we're going to have a fight on our hands, aren't we?'

The guard wilted at the sound of this. He did not seem to be a very strong Spencer-partisan. 'You fellers get bottled up in here and they'll riddle the damned place to get you. Listen; I'll give you my word that if you'll let me go, I won't say a thing. I'll—'

Deming sounded almost disgusted when he said, 'Forget it. An extra hostage won't hurt our chances.'

The nighthawk, known to Ed Teel as a corral-yard hostler for the stage company, and also a slovenly and lazy individual, probably would have kept his word. Ed felt a little sorry for him so he said, 'Don't do anything foolish, Frank, and you'll live to tell your grandchildren about this night.'

Frank did not believe that. 'Marshal, Mister Spencer'd shoot me right along with you fellers if he found me in here with you. He ain't like he used to be. Not any more.'

Ed acknowledged that dryly. 'He sure as hell isn't.'

Hampton was taller than the nighthawk but on this kind of a dark and eerie night he could pass as the nighthawk if he were where that individual was supposed to be, dressed like him, and if he slouched a little.

He looked over where Hugh Deming was sitting on a chair beside the cooling stove. 'Put some wood in,' he told the rancher, 'prop your leg up, and pray.' Hampton smiled at the other two. 'Keep an eye on Frank here, and hope to hell Spencer comes home alone.'

Hampton stepped back outside, eased the door closed without latching it, and looked around for the most likely place to take up his vigil.

The cold was at its worst now, an hour or two before dawn, and Hampton's feet and legs were stiff from the snow that still clung to his boots and trouser-legs from ploughing through the snowbank, but he had one warm hand inside the nighthawk's heavy coat on a warm pistol, and under the circumstances that was about all the reassurance he could count on.

CHAPTER 17

A Worsening Situation

Hampton knew what a warm room could do to men who had been out in the cold for any length of time, men who had not slept in the last fifteen or sixteen hours and were now seated in a warm, dark room, able to relax a little.

For himself, there was little reason to turn drowsy. If the bitter cold did not discourage it, his predicament would. As he walked out a short distance to the protection of a coach, and leaned there where he commanded the best view of the roadway yonder, he almost smiled when he thought how his perfect bank robbery had turned into an unbelievable nightmare. He, who seldom in his life, had felt dependance upon others, had rarely got into positions where he needed allies, was dependent, now, upon two men whom he scarcely knew, who were actually opposed to him for what he'd done.

It was difficult to imagine how a man might complicate his life anymore, and he'd managed it all simply by riding into a high-meadow cow-town to have new shoes put on a bay horse.

Anybody who said a man didn't contribute to his own destiny, or who said there was no such thing as a rule of retribution, didn't know what he was talking about!

Hampton felt like making a smoke but he refrained. It wasn't important anyway, just something to do to help kill time.

He was tempted to go forward to the entranceway and look down through town; if Spencer had his searchers out by now, they were being very discreet because so far Hampton hadn't heard a sound. More probably, with the possible exception of a few men like Meachem, men who either had personal reasons for wanting to find the fugitives, or who were sufficiently under Abel Spencer's influence to do as he said, most of the townsmen would be reluctant, not only because of the congealing cold, but also because no man in his right mind went voluntarily searching in the darkness for three armed and desperate fugitives.

Daylight would of course change that. Hampton speculated a little on their situation if they did not get their hostage, and daylight arrived. About all they could do would be continue to hide, only this time in Spencer's building.

186

He heard someone coming down the roadway. Although the crunching sound was clear, when no one appeared Hampton decided it was the cold and stillness that allowed this footfall-sound to travel so far ahead of the man who was making it.

Hampton moved closer to the coach in order to have an adequate background, drew the gun from inside his borrowed jacket and waited, breath billowing like steam with every beat of his heart. The sound came on without changing, and when it appeared that the unseen walker out beyond the corral-yard had to be close, a soft call floated out of the more distant night, and the footsteps stopped. Someone else was out there, evidently over across the road on the opposite walkway. This latter individual hastened to Hampton's side of the road. He heard those two men conferring and strained to distinguish words, but the voices were too low; in spite of the clearness of the air, they reached Hampton only as a low, rolling murmur.

Hampton turned slowly and peered around the big yard. It was empty. He looked towards the back entrance to Abel Spencer's building, and finally looked towards the open gateway again, as those voices stopped. His guess was that those were some of Spencer's searchers, out there. He hoped very hard one of them would be Spencer. He also hoped if one of them *was* Spencer, he would not bring the second man into the yard with him. Then the echoing footfalls began again as someone came up towards the corral-yard opening. There was only one set of sounds this time, which should have relieved Hampton, but it didn't because now he wondered why the other man hadn't gone back across the road, hadn't at least moved in *some* direction; if he had, Hampton would have heard him. It was not possible to walk anywhere on this particular night and not create sound.

The oncoming footfalls stopped again, just short of the gateway opening. Now, Hampton, was worried. Whoever he was, out there, he was acting as though he knew someone might be waiting for him inside the yard. Hampton grew tense from waiting. It troubled him very much that he could not anticipate whatever strategy those two probable enemies were undertaking. He was too far from the building to cross over there, and doubtless the men inside the gloom were relying on Hampton; they would not walk out to look around.

Finally, he heard the second man; he was moving very stealthily down the side of the southward palisaded fence. Hampton had no time to wonder why those two had become suspicious; perhaps they actually were not really suspicious at all, perhaps they had guessed what the fugitives might attempt. Perhaps they had found the tell-tale tracks in the alley north of the jailhouse. It would require no great acumen to read the sign in all that snow; three men making five tracks could only mean Hampton, Teel, and one-legged Hugh Deming.

Whatever the reason, Hampton was being stalked. He was certain his stalkers did not really know he was waiting for them inside the yard. That gave him some advantage. On the other hand if they forced him into a position where he had to use his gun, not only would he lose his advantage, he would also ensure that a howling mob would soon congregate outside Spencer's building. He had no illusions about the results if he and his companions were cornered, were involved in a shoot-out.

The man out front suddenly walked into plain sight over in the roadway entrance to the corral-yard. Hampton saw him plainly, saw that he was carrying a shotgun cradled in his arms. What he could not determine because the man was bundled against the cold with his hat pulled low and his lower face tucked inside a turned-up furry collar was whether the man was Spencer or someone else. Right at the moment he did not really care, because that other man was still making quiet little crunching footfalls as he slipped down the fence to get behind the coach where Hampton stood like stone, waiting to see if the man facing him out in the roadway entrance discerned a man-shape in the yard.

Evidently he didn't because he entered the yard and turned to gaze towards the building. Hampton breathed a little easier; the coach behind him had snow atop it, icicles down the side, and the dark blur of its near-side formed a blending background, as long as Hampton did not move. In this kind of a situation, where everything was utterly still and silent, movement or sound would give him away, and he knew it.

The unseen stalker finally stopped tracking, over beyond the fence. Hampton guessed he would be entering the yard, back by some horse stalls near the west end of the corral yard. That put the second man behind both Hampton and the coach, but it did not make Hampton feel any better, being invisible from back there, because he was now between a shotgun, in front, and probably a rifle or sixgun, in back.

He waited, scarcely daring to breathe for fear the man out front would catch sight of his steamy breath. Moments later the man out back began moving as quietly as he could down towards the rear door of the building on Hampton's left, and as soon as the first man saw his friend, or heard him coming, he grew bolder and also headed in that direction, but on an angle that carried him towards a northerly junctioin with the second stalker. Hampton estimated where they would meet, and was relieved that it would be well within his sight. He had to turn a little to keep them in sight when they reached one another, but now he was able to plan what course to follow. He was, again, in control of the initiative. So far, neither of those searchers knew Hampton was anywhere close.

A dog barked over on the east side of town, and southward. The man with the shotgun whirled and stood, head-cocked, listening. Evidently some other searcher had roused the animal. The dog continued to bark, but when that was the only sound the man with the shotgun turned back, waiting for his partner to come ahead.

Hampton began to twist from the waist, very slowly. He probably would not have been seen anyway, because the man in his sight was concentrating on his companion, approaching from the rear of the yard. Finally, as that second searcher came around the front of Hampton's coach, he was in plain view.

Hampton ticked off the seconds until those two were close enough to start whispering, then he took down a big breath, let it out very slowly, raised his sixgun and without saying a word cocked the gun. That little sound of steel over steel was better than any command. It carried perfectly in the icy air. The man with the shotgun noticeably stiffened but otherwise he stood perfectly still. His friend, however, started to whirl, to dig under his coat for his sixgun.

Hampton cautioned him in a soft tone of voice. 'Don't try it!'

The man stopped moving, then withdrew his right hand very slowly and let it dangle. He was looking towards the coach where Hampton's voice had come from, but until there was movement over there, he probably could not make Hampton out.

That dog stopped barking and silence settled again throughout Mandan, but obviously the town was crawling with Spencer's organized searchers.

Hampton stepped out where he was visible. He walked ahead a yard or two and gave an order. 'Drop the scatter-gun.' As soon as this had been done, he told his prisoners to reach under, very carefully, and also drop their six-guns. Finally, with their surprise diminishing, one of the men said, 'You are as good as dead, cowboy. The only chance you got is to tell us where them other two are, and maybe Mister Spencer'll figure you helped us and let you off easier.'

Hampton said nothing, but he knew now that he did not have Abel Spencer, only a couple more of his posse-men. He was both disappointed and troubled. These men were certain to be missed, after a while, and since Spencer and his friends knew in which direction these two had been searching, they would also figure out where the fugitives were hiding. But it could not be helped.

When two sixguns dropped to the frozen ground Hampton gestured towards the back of the nearby building with his gunbarrel. 'Single-file,' he ordered, 'and both hands in plain sight. When you get to the door, stop.'

That latter command had been a precautionary measure, but as it turned out it was unnecessary, because Ed Teel suddenly appeared in the opened doorway, gun in hand. As the prisoners clambered through the snow-bank and halted in front of him, Ed looked at them closely, then said, 'Where's Abel?'

One of the searchers answered in a disgusted

voice. 'How the hell would we know, Ed? Last I seen, he was down at the jailhouse givin' orders.' As the prisoner paused, his companion, evidently a man more concerned with his own welfare than anything else, spoke out.

'Listen, Marshal, we only agreed to help out because Abe's making a big manhunt out of this. We weren't going to shoot on sight no matter what Abe said.' This man looked over his shoulder at the menacing silhouette of Hampton back there, his dark eyes narrowed, his mouth flattened in an uncompromising manner. 'No sense in hitting me over the head, Marshal. I'll tell you for a fact, Henry Meachem's got a gash as long as your finger. I'll do whatever you say. All right?'

Teel did not answer. He stepped back and motioned the fresh prisoners inside, then, as Hampton came up, Ed looked up and shook his head in disgust, clearly disappointed that they hadn't caught Abel Spencer.

But there was little they could do about that, now, so they both entered the warm courtroom where Deming, his leg propped out front, sat next to the glowing stove. Someone had the door of the stove open so that the fire inside threw light outward into the room, as well as heat, and a little smoke.

Hampton remained back by the door and

when Ed turned towards him he said, 'This only puts us in deeper. They'll miss these two directly and come lookin' for them.'

The prisoners, all three of them, listened closely to what was being said from a huddle over along the far wall. Deming was holding a sixgun loosely in one hand, keeping an eye on them.

Ed stepped closer to Hampton so they could confer in a low whisper. In Ed's view Abel Spencer was the key to their salvation. He believed they still had to get him, somehow, and he believed that now, with three prisoners that would be missed, they could not simply sit and wait for Spencer to return to his office.

Hampton listened, privately agreeing, but as he said, with the town full of stalking searchers, even if they were certain Spencer was still down at the jailhouse, the chances of anyone catching him alone and off-guard were damned slim. And if he or Ed bungled the attempt, there was no doubt about it, they would never be able to get back to the corral-yard alive.

CHAPTER 18

The First Fatality!

Hampton was not enthusiastic. He appreciated the need for a hostage exactly as he had favoured taking the initiative to the extent of abandoning the attic above Hank's blacksmithing works and coming north to Spencer's building, but he told Ed the odds were very much against them being able to get Spencer, and live through the attempt.

Ed did not argue, he simply took Hampton over where Hugh Deming sat, and, with Deming listening in, he said, 'There's no choice. These damned prisoners are going to be missed. All Abe's waiting for is some idea where we're hiding, then he's going to come down here with all the guns in town.'

Deming put a saturnine look toward Hampton. 'He's right. Not necessarily about the guns, but about the choice. From now on, we're treading water. I wouldn't even want to bet much money that if we had Spencer it'd keep the town from attacking us in here. But at least it's a chance, and the other way we don't have even a prayer.'

Hampton was not that hard to convince. He had not been *against* the idea of trying to abduct Spencer, he just hadn't been enthusiastic about their chances. With a fatalistic look he asked if Deming thought he could keep tabs on their three prisoners while Ed went with Hampton. Deming made a cold little grin. 'No problem at all, and even if they get you boys, I'll still be safe because I'll have something to trade for my life. Don't you worry about me keeping these three neutralized.'

Ed went for his coat and as he was putting it on one of their prisoners said, 'Marshal, Abe's got teams all over the place. You won't get fifty yards from here.'

Ed was buttoning the coat as he said, 'Any suggestions?' and the hostage answered promptly.

'Yeah. Fort up in here and be ready, because within an hour it'll be daylight, and by then we'll be missed. If you're not in here when they come, this feller with the busted leg will never be able to hold 'em off.'

Ed studied the dull faces over against the wall, in flickering firelight, then turned without a word and followed Hampton outside where the cold hit him hard, made him breathe shallowly until his lungs got accustomed to it.

Hampton turned towards the front roadway. As long as they were committed, it was his opinion that they stood their best chance of succeeding if they could pass as searchers.

He had scarcely reached the roadway out yonder, with Ed coming along close behind, than a man appeared from the dark runway between two buildings across the way, and raised a gloved hand in salute. Hampton waved back with complete nonchalance, but before that searcher over there could decide to cross the road to talk, Ed bumped Hampton and turned to walk briskly southward. Hampton fell in and said, 'Suppose we picked up a couple of those men for shields and barged into the jailhouse by the front door.'

Teel did not answer, he simply pointed to the discernible front of the jailhouse. At least four men were clubbed up, down there, talking very earnestly, and carbines glinted dully in the starlight. If there were four or five men outside, there were probably that many inside with Abe Spencer.

Ed faded to his right when they came to another of those dark, narrow places between two buildings. He led Hampton out to the back alley. There, at least, they encountered no one.

Ed started for the rear of his jailhouse. Shortly before reaching the steel-banded oaken rear door, a man sauntered in from over to the west of town where he must have been patrolling among residences. He saw Ed and Hampton and did as the other searcher had done, he waved. But this man was crunching over the snow directly towards the jailhouse even before he had seen what he assumed were other searchers in the back-alley, so he kept right on walking.

There was no time for a conference, even if one had been required. Ed smiled, waved, and acted as though he were waiting for the stranger to come forward, and Hampton dropped his head so the hatbrim shielded his face, turned slightly away, eased out his sixgun then turned back, and as the newcomer came up, Hampton raised the gun with a soft, quiet little warning. 'Not a damned sound!'

The searcher was too astonished to move, for a moment, and that was what Ed had counted on. He moved close, spun the man and struck him down with a pistol-barrel. He then got Hampton to help him drag the limp form to the back door of the jailhouse. He unlocked that door silently, using a brass key from his personal key-ring, motioned Hamptpon in first, to give him cover, then he hauled the unconscious man into the warm darkness of the cell-area, shoved the man's Colt inside his waist-band, and tiptoed forward with Hampton to the closed cell-room door up ahead. Light came under it, and a man's droning voice sounded through it.

Hampton tried to make out if there were other men in the next room, but the only voice was that droning one. Whoever that was would be speaking to at least one other man. He might also be speaking to a roomful of other men. Hampton raised his gun in one hand and reach-ed for the latch with the other hand. He looked back just once. Ed nodded.

'Open it.'

Hampton grasped the latch firmly, lifted it without a sound, then shoved the door open very fast and stepped forth.

There were three men in the room, next to Spencer and the man nearest him was Henry Meachem with a rag round his head and a car-bine across his knees. The third man was younger than either Spencer or Meachem, and he reached first. Astonishment held the pair of older men rooted to their chairs, but the younger man came up half off his bench along the wall, clawing for his sixgun.

Ed called out sharply. 'Jasper! Don't try it!'

The young man, gun half-clear, froze. Hampton had him covered, had cocked his sixgun. The young man was a hair's breadth away from Eternity. He wilted.

Abe Spencer's face got twisted with fury or fear, or perhaps some of both, but Meachem, already with a headache, very aware that those two armed men in front of him had reason to hate him, remained impassive and motionless.

Hampton's gun swung towards Spencer. 'On your feet!'

Spencer leaned at the desk and glared, but did not obey. Hampton started forward and Spencer recoiled behind the desk. Hampton smiled, his black eyes like hard obsidian. 'You bastard, I'd just as soon kill you right here. *Stand up.*'

This time Spencer obeyed. Hampton reached, caught hold of Spencer and wrenched him violently from behind the desk, then he flung the sixgun away into a corner leaving Spencer's holster empty, turned his prisoner and gave him a violent shove towards Ed Teel. Meachem had hardly even looked up throughout this little interlude, but when Hampton shoved his gun-barrel into Meachem's throat and held out a hand, Meachem obediently surrendered his carbine. Probably because he thought he knew what was to happen next, Meachem begged.

'I won't make a sound for five minutes. *Ten* minutes. Just don't hit me on the head again.'

Hampton laughed, and struck. Meachem slumped off his chair, his hat having muffled the sound of his being struck down again.

They drove Spencer ahead of them out into the cold back alleyway, and had scarcely made it when someone inside the front jailhouse office, evidently one of those men from out front who had entered just now, let off a bellow that could be heard a hundred yards in all directions. Without any doubt, Meachem's unconscious form had been found, and Spencer's absence had been instantly noted.

Ed told Spencer to head north up the alleyway and to hurry. This time, Abe obeyed without being coerced. But it did not help very much. Hampton was trotting along in the rear when the little mob of armed men burst out of the jailhouse. Those men were armed, and when one of them shouted, then threw up his carbine, Hampton did not hesitate. He fired twice, fast. Down the alley a glass window broke into a hundred fragments, and the second bullet peeled a long splinter from the jailhouse back-wall. Those four men squawked and hurled themselves in every direction to get clear.

This bought a little time, but now men were calling out all over town. Hampton and Teel had no time to confer; no time in fact to do anything but hasten unerringly back in the direction of Spencer's office and courtroom. They were barely visible up the alleyway when one of those scattered possemen back down by the jailhouse let loose with a lever-action salvo that peppered the night with bullets, none even close enough to be heard by the fleeing men.

Abe Spencer's breath made a whistling, wheezing sound as he sped along without additional encouragement from his captors. Whoever that was, back down there shooting northward up the alleyway, could not possibly know who he might hit, and Spencer was just as aware of that as were Hampton and Ed Teel.

Out front, for some unfathomable reason, another man opened up with a carbine. Perhaps he had mistaken another posseman or two for Hampton and Teel. Perhaps he had been hoisting a few to keep his insides warm and was feeling exuberant enough to cut loose just for the hell of it.

Hampton saw Ed veer towards the back of the corral-yard as though he knew there might be a gate back there. Of course there was a gate because one of those men Hampton had captured earlier had entered the yard from the rear, somewhere. But if Ed knew where the gate was, that was more than Hampton knew.

Abel Spencer fell limply against the fence when they found their way through from out back. It hadn't really been that long a race, but through a couple of feet of snow it certainly was; men running under stress for a mile over bare ground would have been just as exhausted, providing they were as soft as Spencer seemed to be.

Hampton reached, caught the prisoner's shoulder and hurled him through the gate. Spencer had to stumble twenty feet ahead before he could regain his balance. From the front entranceway a carbine blasted, its muzzle-blast a licking tongue of orange fire that temporarily blinded both Hampton and Teel, but they both fired back without aiming, and the posseman out there fled loudly down the frozen night. But he yelled as he fled, telling everyone within hearing that he had seen the abductors of Abe Spencer.

No doubt about it, although Ed and Hampton had made it when Hampton had at least doubted they could, and although they had their prized hostage, neither of these things seemed likely to prevent a wild shooting-spree when the possemen got up to where they could surround and besiege Spencer's building.

Ed gripped Spencer's arm and tried to drag the man across through snow the last hundred feet to the back of the building. Spencer acted as though each leg weighed a hundred pounds, he moved ahead, but dumbly, without even looking to see where he was going. Hampton had to reach Spencer on the far side, grip his middle and half-push, half-carry, him to the doorway.

Inside, when Hampton jumped aside upon entering, as a precaution, Hugh Deming was sitting over by the stove, still with his broken leg propped out front, red fireglow making his face and features mephistopheleian in a sweat-shiny way. He even made a cold smile at sight of Abel Spencer.

The hostages, sitting now, were otherwise still over against the far wall using the same bench Hank had used during the mock-trial. They seemed surprised, not just to find Abe Spencer in the room, like them, a captive, but also astonished to find that Hampton and Teel had lived through all the gunfire they had been able to hear, out in the brittle-cold night.

Spencer reached a chair and sagged into it. His head dropped so far forward he had to raise both hands to cradle it. In the momentary hush everyone in the ghostly-lighted room could hear his uneven, wheezing breath. Hampton, back by the door peeering out, turned and looked. 'Any whisky in here?' he asked. 'Better get some down that man.' Scarcely had Hampton finished speaking than Abe Spencer's arm dropped away and his entire upper body very slowly eased forward,. He fell from the chair without a sound and lay in a huddled, limp posture that surprised everyone so much that although they all were looking, had all witnessed his fall, no one moved until Ed Teel stepped across and knelt, holstering his sixgun as he reached to straighten Spencer out on the floor.

Ed leaned low, then straightened a little to complete his cursory examination, and finally looked at Hampton as he said, 'By gawd he's dead. There's no heartbeat at all.'

Deming asked a reasonable question. 'Was he hit in the escape?'

Ed opened Spencer's coat and leaned for a close look. There was no wound, anywhere. One of the hostages over on the wall bench said, 'Ed; his heart. You recollect he had a seizure couple years back?'

Teel remembered. He murmured Abe Spencer's obiturary. 'Sure as hell.'

CHAPTER 19

Gunthunder!

Hugh Deming made a perfectly rational statement, that was as wrong as hell. 'That ought to take the fight out of them, Spencer being dead. He was the leader.'

Deming had scarcely finished speaking when gunfire erupted from out back in the corral-yard, and from out front in the roadway. The attackers out back were well hidden among parked vehicles and the horse stalls. The men out front, although they really did not have anything worthwhile to shoot at, unless it was simply the front of Spencer's building, had cover over among the dark buildings opposite.

Hampton looked over at Deming and smiled with bitterness. 'You want to hop out there and tell them Spencer is dead so's they'll quit shooting?'

The hostages over against the wall rolled off their bench to lie flat on the floor when that first fusillade erupted. One of them squawked from a near miss and snake-crawled his way

207

under the bench for additonal protection.

Ed was kneeling by the only rear-wall window trying to see who all was out back when a bullet struck the topmost pane of glass bursting it inward and showering Ed with sharp fragments that his hat largely deflected. At once, frigid night air rushed in. Moments later when a lull came, Deming spoke dryly from his place over beside the stove.

'Nice having that fresh air for a change; it was getting a little stuffy in here.'

Hampton, like the other defenders, had only a handgun. There was a Winchester lying out beyond the nearest snowbank but it might as well have been on the moon. The range, even to the rear of the corral-yard, was a little far for handgun shooting, especially in the kind of paling, lead-belly grey light that predominated out there, as the new day strove to reach Mandan.

Hampton called over to Ed about this, and Teel, back crouching by the window again, said, 'There's a gunrack in the stage-line office out front, but we're not going to need longer barrels as much as we're going to need ammunition. However this ends, it'll be short-range shooting.'

Hampton flinched when someone out back opened up with a heavy rifle, not a carbine, and the slug that struck wood made the entire rear wall quiver under impact. One of the huddling hostages bleated like a ewe, then said, 'That'll be old Dan Kerfman the gunsmith; him and his lousy buffler-gun. Hey, Ed, can't you sing out to them boys?'

By now there were gun-firing attackers on all sides of the building, but to the north there was nothing but a thick, blank wall to fire into so most of the attackers were either out front, out back, or southward somewhere, firing into the equally as solid wooden wall that was the courtroom's southerly wall. Presently, the exuberance of the attackers made it impossible for a man's voice to be heard outside. Ed impatiently waited for a moment when the gunfire would at least diminish enough so that he could call out that Abel Spencer was dead, but not only did that moment seem unlikely to come, after a quarter-hour of this fierce and savage fighting, Ed began to wonder if Spencer, alive or dead, would make any difference.

Hampton returned from out front with two shotguns, two carbines, and a large cardboard carton of sixgun slugs. He left a shotgun with Ed, gave Deming one of the carbines as well as more bullets, then took a position near the door between the courtroom and the office out front. The office had two windows facing the road. Both had been shot to pieces. The door was bolted from the inside, but it was rather flimsy, as most doors went, being made of upright planks reinforced in back with diagonal braces, and every time a bullet struck it a splintery hole appeared on the inside. Even six-gun slugs fired from across the road went through that door. Hampton had decided, while raiding the wall gunrack, that there was no safe way to defend the building from that front office. He now stood well to the south where the doorway led into the rear courtroom, able to see into the eerie, blue-grey haze of the pre-dawn roadway. That was as close as he cared to get to the centre of the office.

Hugh Deming abandoned his warm and comfortable place beside the stove and hobbled back to bend low so that he could also fire from the glassless rear window. The attackers out back were the only ones in the fight, excepting the besieged men inside, who were actually under hostile gunfire, and when Teel suddenly appeared to have an ally firing out the back of the window too, quite a number of those guns back there went silent as their owners skipped away.

A bold spirit made a crouching run in zig-zag fashion from across the northward road towards the front office, and Hampton admired the man's courage as he raised a carbine and fired low, out through one of the glassless windows. The rushing man bawled, fell, then began to frantically roll towards a nearby bank of snow. He disappeared over there.

Hampton checked the loads in his carbine, then turned to look into the courtroom where Teel and Deming were making the corral-yard decidedly uncomfortable for the men back among the stalls and stages. One of the hostages was staring from a low crouch towards the backs of the two defenders at the window. Hampton raised his carbine and waited. Sixth-sense made the prisoner look over his shoulder. He saw that steel barrel fixed on him and winked. Hampton lowered the gun, walked over to that man, and leaned. The hostage guessed what was coming and lunged, not away, but forward, towards Hampton's legs. He took the carbine barrel alongside the head cross one ear. The other hostages were as still as stone when their companion dropped face-forward.

Hampton went back to his doorway without the defenders at the window realizing what had happened.

Dawn arrived and while its gunmetal colour alleviated both the darkness and at least some of the cold, the day did not look as though it were going to be a pleasant one in a lot of ways.

But that was everyone's initial assessment because the misty, gloomy cloudbank that was drifting north-westerly on a diagonal course above Mandan, was solid from horizon to horizon.

It was still very early. As Deming leaned to say loudly to Ed Teel, when the rank of rearward attackers seemed to be thinning out, 'This isn't even a very good day for dyin'.' Deming smiled through his whisker-stubble, then twisted to look back where Hampton was able to watch both rooms, the office out front and the bullet-spattered courtroom in back. He saw the unconscious hostage with the bloody scalp and evidently assuming the man had been a victim of his friends out in the corral-yard, shrugged and turned towards the corpse of Abel Spencer. When Ed, too, looked, Deming said into Ed's ear that it was a damned lousy shame Spencer hadn't had to sit in here with the rest of them and see what it was like, being under the siege he had himself, whipped up.

Ed nodded and leaned to peer cautiously round the window and got a surprise, there was a soft-golden hint of sunshine to the leaden, low and misty overcast. He had time to appreciate it only briefly, then that man with the buffalo rifle cut loose from a horse-stall and a big sliver

212

of wood was torn off the wall directly above. Deming fired at the black-powder puff of smoke with his sixgun, drew up and fired again. Ed heard this firing but he had ducked down as bits of wood pelted him and only thought he heard a loud bellow from out back. Deming drew aside to punch out casings and plug in fresh loads. He was smiling, splinted leg notwithstanding. Because the return-firing was thunderous now, coming from angry men out back, Deming could not make himself heard, so he gestured with a cocked finger to indicate that he had scored a hit.

Ed nodded, only slightly pleased; he had known that old gunsmith, Dan Kerfman, very well. The first booming roar Ed had heard, he knew who that was back there. Perhaps he should have felt outraged, at least indignant, that old Kerfman, with whom he'd spent many a pleasant summer twilight sitting and talking in Kerfman's gunshop, should have allowed himself to be talked into trying to kill Ed now, but all he really felt was disappointment, a kind of disillusioned sadness.

Hampton left his post between the front and back rooms and sidled over near the rearwall window where he dropped to one knee beside Ed and put his head down to speak.

'This is getting worse instead of better,' he

exclaimed. 'There's more idiots out there now, than there was last night. This damned building'll collapse from the weight of lead if they don't let up. How about making a white flag and waving it out the windows. It's light enough now for them to see it.'

Ed liked that suggestion. He beckoned Deming over and the three of them held a brief conference, then Hampton arose to implement his suggestion. His immediate obstacle was that although there were beds, and bedding, upstairs in the rooming-house part of Spencer's building, crossing the front office to climb the stairs was pure suicide. The men across the road were firing into the office as though they had real targets. To Hampton, it was ridiculous, this business of wasting all the ammunition, but there was no denying one thing; anyone attempting to cross to the stairway, if he got hit hard, would be just as dead by accident as on purpose.

Hampton went down behind the stage-line ticket counter looking for a white cloth, any kind of a rag that would serve his purpose. He found nothing until he was at the far end of the counter, only a tantalizing yard or two from those stairs leading upwards where there surely would be sheets and white quilts. There, while he was speculating on a man's chances of racing up the stairs, he sighted something white from the corner of his eye. It was one of those linen dusters men and women wore when they rode in open buggies. It was like a smock, buttoned down the front, and reached just below a wearer's knees. That, Hampton thought, reaching out, would be just what he needed.

The next thing was to tie the white coat to the end of his carbine barrel and shove it out the front window. While he was doing this a rash soul across the road roared out a blisteringly condemnatory denunciation of the men inside Spencer's building, and stood up to shake his carbine. Hampton peered around, saw that man, was tempted, but in the end settled back to his work, then thrust the carbine out and wagged it back and forth.

The gunfire across the roadway diminished reluctantly. For the first time Hampton could see that gunmen were also atop the buildings up and down the roadway. He also noticed something else; another leader had appeared among the attackers, replacing Abel Spencer. Whoever that man was, he seemed to be directing the attack from within the saloon, which was across the road and not very far to Hampton's right. It was this man, calling forth in a deep roar that Hampton's white flag was a trap, that sought to keep his townsmen firing. But he was not quite successful. A few attackers, mostly from out back in the corral-yard where it was not possible to see the white flag, continued to fire their weapons, but after a while, when everyone else stopped shooting, even those hold-outs were compelled to desist. A man's antagonistic cursing caused the final attacker to lower his gun.

Out front, the man in the saloon, hands cupped to make is exhortation carry better, swore and ranted, trying to incite the attackers to keep fighting. As near as Hampton could determine, no one was paying any attention to him.

A strong, flat-toned voice sang out from cover. 'You in there with the white flag—what do you want?'

'And end to this,' replied Hampton, and looked around as Ed Teel, stepping over debris, made his way to the window. Hampton motioned Ed on up. 'Talk to them,' he said.

From across the way that same strong, flat voice spoke again. 'Who says to stop, you fellers the law's after, or Abe Spencer?'

Ed gestured for Hampton to keep silent, and leaned from the window when he answered. 'This is Ed Teel. I'm speaking for Spencer. This is all over now. Send someone to the

216

middle of the road to meet me. There's no damned sense at all in getting more people hurt.'

Hampton saw light glint of blue steel from the saloon's doorway and grabbed Teel violently with one hand and wrenched him away just as that hidden gunman over across the road fired. Wood flew, striking both Hampton and Teel, but the bullet had struck where Ed had been, not where he now was.

Before Hampton could face forward again that man with the hard, flat voice, roared out angrily. 'You damned fool, inside the saloon, we was talking peace... Some of you boys go in there and get that treacherous bastard!'

Ed brushed off wood and looked out. The man in the saloon had evidently withdrawn his gun, had moved away from the door because there was nothing to be seen over there.

From across the road that hard-voiced man called over again, 'Hey, Ed; that was Meachem. He won't do that again. All right, I'll meet you in the centre of the road. If anyone gets trigger-happy the fellers here with me know what to do. You ready?'

Ed answered as he moved up to the window again. 'Yeah.' He didn't use the broken door to leave the building, he simply stepped out through the glassless window.

CHAPTER 20

The Fight Ends

Hugh Deming, propped against the rear wall of the courtroom, was watching the two conscious prisoners working over the groggy man Hampton had struck down. He was tired and dirty, cold and hungry, and his leg hurt like blue blazes. Now that the battle seemed to be finished, he wanted very much to lie down, or sit down, and give his leg a long rest.

Hampton came to a stand in the doorway between the two rooms again, and Deming nodded towards their hostages. 'No trouble here,' he said. 'How's it going out front?'

Ed was in the middle of the road where sunlight reflecting off snow made him squint his eyes nearly closed. With him was a bearded, burly man, whose hair was grey-streaked, and whose face was tough-set in a no-nonsense expression. His name was Art Carpenter and he was Abe Spencer's corral-yard-boss, a man nearly ten years older than Ed Teel with a reputation for being outspoken and hard-headed. He and Ed had known one another for five or six years, and the first thing Art Carpenter said, when they were face-to-face in the roadway was, 'I apologize for Henry, Ed; that was a lousy thing he just done.' Then Carpenter asked about his employer, and as Ed explained what had happened, Carpenter's hard face got harder, as though he doubted Ed's word.

For Teel, who had not expected Spencer's friend and associates to quite believe how Abe had died, there was one benefit to be derived from taking those three hostages. He turned now, and called for Hampton to send them out. While he waited he told Carpenter the captives had witnessed Abe's fatal seizure, and finally, Carpenter seemed to accept the truth. But as he did so, he flopped his thick arms and looked around at the bullet-marked buildings and at the waiting armed men behind him, then he spoke, sounding disgusted, or perhaps demoralized.

'How the hell could this happen, here in Mandan? What made me back Abe like I done?'

Ed made no attempt to answer, but as the two unarmed men, helping the third hostage, walked forward from the building behind Ed, he said, 'Anyone killed on your side, Art?' and when Carpenter shook his head before turning to scowl at the oncoming hostages, Ed told him that no one had been injured in the stage-line building either, so, as the crestfallen hostages came up and halted, Ed summed up the battle in a few prophetic words.

'Well; I reckon no one'll ever come up with the right answer, Art, but at least we won't have to attend any funerals.'

Carpenter growled at the hostages. 'You boys see Abe die?'

Two of the hostages told their story. It verified everything Ed Teel had told him. The third man, the one Hampton had hit over the head, only nodded. He did not feel very good. Carpenter told his friends to take him down to the saloon and pour a little forty-rod medicine down him. Carpenter then flapped his arms again, looking exasperatedly at Ed. 'Well; at least I done one right thing last night,' he said. 'When Abe sent some of us after your brother with orders to gun him down if he made trouble, I knocked Hank cold before he knew what was up so's the other lads wouldn't get trigger-happy, and carried him to the jailhouse. He's still locked up, down there; got a jaw on him the size of an apple.'

Men began appearing up and down the plankwalks on both sides of the roadway where warm sunshine began to turn snow into run-off water. While Carpenter and Ed Teel were turning, side by side, to go to the west side of the road, a lanky older man with a great cud of chewing tobacco pushing the right side of his face out of shape, strolled over and held out a hand to Ed. On this man's palm was the town marshal's badge. The lanky man spat aside, then spoke in the soft drawl of west Texas. 'Found it atop the bar. Reckon Henry pitched it there.' The lanky man spat aside again and squinted down the southward roadway. 'Barman said Henry run for his horse and lit out o'town. Bad ridin' weather, but if you figure we'd ought to fetch him back, Marshal Teel, I'd be right obliged to go after him.'

Art Carpenter gave the answer Ed was about to give. 'Let him go. Damn him anyway. Mandan's a sight better off without Henry Meachem...' Carpenter scowled into the southward distance as he paused. 'Better off without Abe too, I reckon, but when I'm takin' a man's money I don't set in judgement on him.'

They turned as Hampton came out of the battered building where he and Hugh Deming were the last two hold-outs. Hampton waited until Deming, using a broken chair as his support, moved forth where sunshine was, then Hampton tipped his hatbrim down against sun-glare and let Deming come on up even with him before they both started southward.

Art Carpenter stared for a while, then mumbled under his breath about Deming really having a broken leg. Ed knew that Carpenter had believed Spencer's lie about Deming pretending to be injured, but he said nothing.

Mandan looked entirely different in broad daylight than it had looked all the previous night. It was warmer, too, and although melting snow made the roadway a quagmire of brown gumbo, as yet people were so pleased at the prospect of a return of warm weather that they did not complain. By the following day, though, they would be grumbling, because by then the mud would be impossible to keep out of homes and stores, what with the snow melting fast, as the heat continued to rise. Evidently Indian summer was going to return, was going to remain for a few more weeks.

Mostly, people avoided Ed Teel and his rumpled, unshaven, sunken-eyed companions. Most people were too chagrined at being taken in by Abel Spencer. Hank, as soon as they let him out of the jailhouse cell, said he had a score to settle with someone, and would have gone in search of Art Carpenter, except that Hampton blocked him at the jailhouse doorway, smilingly obdurate.

'Forget it, can't you?' he said. 'Me, I've had all the trouble I need for the rest of my life. You ought to feel the same way, Hank. Anyway, that old boy with the whiskers did you a favour.'

Ed verified this, so Hank subsided, but as Art Carpenter had said, Hank had a swollen jaw; it was the pain caused by this that kept him from getting very involved in the conversation in the jailhouse. Finally, when Deming asked if someone would go find him something to eat, Hank could participate. Hampton too, was half-starved, but he needed something more than just food. Hank promised to fetch back a bottle of that too.

Alone again, the three of them got comfortable in the little jailhouse office. Hampton made a smoke in silence. Deming and Ed Teel watched him do this, also in silence. Later, when Hampton had the cigarette lighted, had looked up to see the way he was being stared at, he understood perfectly what was in the minds of his fighting-partners.

He blew out a grey cloud. 'A man's supposed to be glad just to be alive after he's spent a night like we spent isn't he?'

Neither of the other men answered. They simply sat easy, gazing at Hampton.

The black eyes brightened with a hard smile.

'All right. I'm alive, and I reckon I'm glad about that. You fellers want me to ride out and fetch back my saddlebags?'

Deming had evidently given this some weighty thought because he said, 'Yeah. No sense in either of us going with you. I can't ride too well and Ed's tail feathers are drooping. Can you make it out there and back through the snow?'

Hampton nodded. 'It's not all that far.'

Deming accepted this as though the idea of Hampton taking the saddlebags, and his freshly shod bay horse, and keeping right on riding, hadn't crossed his mind. 'You still figure to see California, or wherever it was you were heading for?'

Hampton considered the rancher impassively. 'What you got in mind, Mister Deming?'

'Ride out, cowboy. Hand over the saddlebags and keep right on going southward. Those folks up in Montana want their money back and you don't blame them for that any more'n I do. On the other hand, with Marhsal Teel's approval, it seems to me you've sure as hell earned the right to keep on going.'

Ed was agreeable. Perhaps, if he'd been a professional lawman he might have viewed this situation differently, but by profession Ed Teel was a liveryman. He had always said that he was not a very good law officer and the way he felt today, after seeing half the town against him without a really valid reason, he had just about made up his mind to hand in his badge at the very next meeting of the Town Council.

Hampton arose. The three men looked at one another a moment, then Ed smiled. 'Glad I don't have to make that ride out and back with you,' he said.

Hampton went out the door as Hank came in it, carrying a bottle tucked under one arm and three tin plates of hot stew balanced in his two hands. He turned as though to call Hampton back, but Ed interrupted.

'Let him go. He'll be back directly anyway. Hank, is that all you could dig up, beef stew again?'

Hank looked indignant as he put the plates atop Ed's desk. 'It's not *beef* stew, it's *elk* stew, which is ten times tougher, and if you don't like it there's no law says you have to eat it.'

Deming twisted the cap of the whisky bottle and took a long pull before taking one of the tin plates in his lap. Both he and Ed were ravenous, but it was that kind of hunger that men aren't aware of for as long as they are in peril; but afterwards, that kind of hunger replaced every other emotion and made them eat like horses.

Hank stoked up the stove, but it was getting almost warm enough without a fire, and outside people were flocking the plankwalks. Hank said at least ten townsmen and their womenfolk had come up to tell him they'd taken no part in Spencer's madness. This inclined Deming to make a tart comment.

'Sure. And as the months pass fewer and fewer folks will be saying that, until no more'n a handful will have been shooting at us, and for my part, I'll always be mystified how so damned few people could have shot so damned many guns.'

Ed remembered something. 'Hank; what about old Dan Kerfman?'

'Busted leg,' the blacksmith retorted, reaching for the whisky bottle. 'Same leg, in fact, as Mister Deming. There's another feller with one; he was trying to cross the road during the battle and someone nailed him from inside the stage office. Otherwise, except for a bad scare or two, no one got hurt. Which reminds me: from in my cell it sounded like the Battle of the Little Bighorn out there. How in hell can so many men throw that much lead and not cause more injuries?'

Ed offered an explanation between mouthfuls. 'Lousy light, too much good cover for everyone, and it was so damned cold my teeth were clattering every time I pulled a trigger. Also—lousy marksmen.'

Deming smiled. He'd been about to suggest the latter.

Hank had heard about Meachem leaving town in a rush. He had also heard from the clerk over at the general store that Art Carpenter had taken over the stage company's Mandan depot, and that he'd hired a man to make a decent coffin for Abel Spencer. It was while he was explaining this, a matter of about two hours after Deming and Ed Teel had finished eating, that a horseman rode up out front and leaned down from the saddle to call.

'Hey, Ed.'

Deming and Teel exchanged a look, both had reason to know that voice, Ed arose and stepped out upon the plankwalk where ice-cold drops of snow-water from the overhang eaves fell into the muddy-roadway in an almost continuous stream.

Hampton held out the fat saddlebags. They were dark from moisture. As Ed took them Hampton said. 'You'd better look inside.'

Ed slung the bags over one shoulder. 'Why? It's all there, isn't it?'

Hampton smiled at his little teasing joke. 'Yeah. But if town'd been another half mile I might have weakened.'

Ed admired the handsome bay horse, and when Hampton saw this he said, 'I reckon I've got to re-steal him because I don't have anything to buy him with.'

From the doorway where he leaned, Deming held out a folded paper for Ed to hand to the mounted man. 'Bill-of-sale for one bay thoroughbred marked HRD on the neck, marked paid in full.' As Ed took the paper to hand it up, Deming spoke again. 'Come back some day, cowboy, and look me up. I've always got a job for a good man, summer or winter.'

Hampton's smile lingered. 'Mister Deming, I sure appreciate that, but you know, right now if I never see Montana, Colorado or Wyoming again, it's going to be too soon. Me and the bay horse are going to find us a place where the sun shines three hundred days out of the year, where we can homestead us a hundred and sixty acres, sew a little oats for him, maybe plant a little corn and beans for me—and we're not even going to *look* at another bank as long as we live.'

Hampton lifted the reins, the bay horse responded eagerly after standing for so long in a stall, and the two men in front of the jailhouse watched horse and man go slogging down through the mud where the north-south roadway lay, beginning to show bare, muddy places again.

Ed turned to hand the saddlebags to Hugh Deming. They stepped back inside the jailhouse for another pull at the whisky bottle, and unsuspecting Hank opened one of the saddlebags, peered inside, then hauled straight up as though he had seen a coiled rattlesnake. 'Good Lord a'mighty, there's a fortune in here. These things are stuffed with money!'

Ed and Deming exchanged a wink, then sat down to enjoy a relaxing, quiet drink. In many ways they had both just lived through half a lifetime. It took some quiet and comfortable reflection to make all the adjustments to something like that, each of them would want to make.

It helped greatly, too, that after being cold for so long, they could now feel real heat from the sun again.

MAGNA-THORNDIKE hopes you have enjoyed this Large Print book. All our Large Print titles are designed for easy reading, and all our books are made to last. Other Magna Print or Thorndike Press books are available at your library, through selected bookstores, or directly from the publishers. For more information about current and upcoming titles, please call or mail your name and address to:

MAGNA PRINT BOOKS
Long Preston, Near Skipton,
North Yorkshire,
England BD23 4ND
(07294) 225

or in the USA

THORNDIKE PRESS
P.O. Box 159
Thorndike, Maine 04986
(800) 223-6121
(207) 948-2962
(in Maine and Canada call collect)

There is no obligation, of course.

A

THE GUNS OF HIGH MEADOW
Buck Standish

The fugitive had planned so carefully that the people who wanted him in Montana had no idea which direction he'd taken. Then he rode into Mandan, Colorado, to have a stolen horse shod, and was apprehended for horsestealing. A hate-filled stage company manager schemed to have the fugitive lynched.
Ed Teel, took the fugitive with him to save a lost and injured traveller. The very next day all hell broke loose, Ed was also branded an outlaw, as was the man they had rescued, and only desperation and fast guns kept him alive until it was possible to set things to rights again.

Magna Print Books

Long Preston, Nr. Skipton, N. Yorkshire.

Distributed in North America By:–

THORNDIKE PRESS

P.O. BOX 159, THORNDIKE, ME. 04986

ISBN 1 85057 903 2 (Soft Cover)